MY ENEMY, MY LOVE

Letters From the Past Series

TINA CLOUGH

MY ENEMY, MY LOVE

Copyright © Tina Clough 2023

The author asserts her moral right to be identified as the author of this work.

PAPERBACK ISBN 978-1-99-118715-4

A catalogue record of this book is available from the National Library of New Zealand

Lightpool Publishing

www.lightpoolpublishing.com

Cover and book design by Andrene Low

Chapter 1

After the service Gemma took charge as Jamie stood hesitating outside the church, blinking in the late summer sunshine. 'Let's go for a drink!' she said and hooked her arm through Jamie's. 'I know the pub just opened, but I think a drink is called for. Let's give your mum a proper little wake – just the two of us. We'll go to that pub with the sexy barmaid, she's such a character.'

Jamie was relieved that Gemma was prepared to take charge and had generously taken the whole day off to go to the funeral and keep her company.

'For a moment there I couldn't think what I was supposed to do. I know it seems strange, but I couldn't bear to go to the crematorium and see the coffin disappear into that oven. I'd rather remember the flowers and the light through the stained-glass windows in the church. Did you notice the golden beam of light falling right on the coffin?'

'I did, it was very pretty. And did *you* notice that the

vicar's bald patch shone with a halo when that golden beam fell on him?'

Jamie grinned. 'No, I didn't notice the halo, but OK, let's go. The sexy barmaid is just what I need.'

The bar was quiet and cool. The sexy barmaid stood at the far end of the bar looking out the window with a crease between her eyebrows. She turned when she heard them. 'Some people!' she said indignantly. 'They have no idea, do they? Why do they have kids if they can't be bothered being kind to them?'

Gemma slid Jamie a sideways glance of amusement and said, 'I couldn't agree more. But we've just come from the funeral for my friend's mother, and we need a drink.'

'I'm sorry to hear that,' said the sexy barmaid to Jamie. 'Was she a kind mother?'

'She was very kind. I was an only child with no father and my childhood was happy. I was lucky. What were you looking at through the window?'

The barmaid leaned over the bar and pointed further up the street with her sexy attributes generously displayed in her lowcut top. 'See that girl in the blue sweatshirt? She's got this little kid – I can't see him from here, but he's only two or three. And she's forever dragging him away when he spots something interesting on the ground, nearly pulls his arm out of its socket. They walk past nearly every day, and the poor kid is just interested in things, but he's never allowed to stop and look. One of these days I'll go out and give her a piece of my mind.'

'Maybe she's in a hurry,' said Gemma, who wanted this conversation to finish so they could order their drinks.

'Ha!' said the barmaid darkly. 'Not her, she's got nothing to be in a hurry about, been on one benefit or another since she left school. Now, what would you like to drink?'

Gemma took control and ordered two gin and tonic, and Jamie laughed. 'Honestly, Gemma! I don't think I've ever my life drunk gin before lunchtime.'

'It's a special day, isn't it?' said the barmaid. 'You've got to see your mum off in style, a glass of Coke wouldn't do it.'

Gemma led the way to a table at the far side of the room. 'This should do it – we don't want her to be part of the conversation the whole time we're here.' She reached across the little table and put her hand on Jamie's. 'I was surprised there were so few people at the church. You did put the notice in the paper, didn't you?'

'Oh yes, but I didn't expect many to turn up. I mean, she only moved here after she retired and then just a year later, she started getting dementia and I don't think she went out a lot after that. She didn't have time to make many new friends. I never understood why she didn't stay in Taunton where she had tons of friends, it seemed such an odd thing to do. But she really wanted to come back here, to the area where she grew up. It might have been to do with her illness. Dementia is such a mysterious thing. Not that we knew she had it then, but it was probably developing. And once she went into the care-home and got so much worse I think her few friends just stopped visiting.'

'I feel guilty now that I didn't go to see her more often.' Gemma let go of Jamie's hand and lifted her glass. 'Here's to Heather - a good mother! Have some nuts, darling, it's only quarter to eleven and we don't want to trip over our feet on the way home or perhaps we should order tapas. I kept thinking I would go and see her, but I felt so insecure. I mean, would she recognise me, or would I just cause confusion – you know? And how to do you have a conversation when the other person can't remember what you said two minutes ago? If I'd known her for longer, it would have been easier, but I wimped out.'

Jamie smiled at Gemma's worried frown. 'I know, and believe it or not, I felt the same way. Towards the end I don't think she recognised me. Sometimes she thought I was a caregiver, and once she thought I was her sister, who's been dead for forty years. Before I moved here, I didn't really understand how far down that path she'd gone, because she was great at covering up when we talked on the phone. She pretended she knew what we were talking about and kind of repeated things I'd just said. It was only when I was visiting and could see her face, that I noticed she sometimes looked as if she had no idea what was going on.'

'William was sorry he had to be in court this morning, he usually manages to go to his clients' funerals. Not that she was a client, exactly, but she did ask him to look after that letter he mentioned the other night. He said it's sitting on his desk waiting for you to pick it up.'

Jamie had only known Gemma for the two years since she moved to Kingsbridge to live closer to her mother. They met when Heather told her that she had left something with a local solicitor for Jamie to have after Heather's death. 'Just some papers,' Heather had said vaguely. 'I'll show you where his office is, I can't remember his name.'

This idea was forgotten until one day, when they went out for coffee, Heather pointed across the street and said, 'That's the place!' and insisted on going in. 'I'll know which one he is when I see the names beside the door.'

They spent ten minutes with kind and patient William, who seemed to have a natural talent for talking to people who forget where they were and why they had come.

'She probably brought you in to remind you of the letter she gave me to hold for you,' said William to Jamie, when Heather started humming quietly to herself. 'Mrs Jamieson gave it to me a while ago, but I have instructions to keep it until ... ahem, until after your mother's demise, so you can't have it now.'

They both glanced at Heather, who was looking out the window and paying no attention to the conversation and smiled at each other. Jamie didn't correct him, but her mother was never married. Jamie was born after what Heather had referred to as 'an infatuation' when Jamie as a teenager asked who her father was. She has always assumed this meant that her mother had a one-night stand and never knew the name of the man, but sometimes, in moments of teenage lust for drama, she had speculated that her father was a murderer or a bank robber and Heather didn't want her to know bad things about him. When William politely saw them out, they met his wife Gemma coming in, introductions were made, and Gemma and Jamie had been friends ever since.

'Tell William I'll pick it up soon,' she said now to Gemma. 'God knows, it's probably just some family papers or something. She was an old mother, as you know, and her parents were both dead before I turned three.' She smiled affectionately at Gemma's concerned face. 'It's not as if it's going to be something worth money, she truly had nothing at the end. She had some kind of pension that paid a nice little amount monthly, but it had just stopped paying about the time I came here. That's why I took those evening shifts at The Anchorage – so I could afford to pay for some extras both while she was in the flat and then at the care home. She liked having her hair coloured regularly, things like that. I sold nearly all her furniture when she went into care, too. Some of it I gave away, the stuff that wasn't worth anything.'

'Not that gorgeous Regency sideboard? I never thought to ask you about it when you emptied out Heather's flat, but surely you kept that!'

'Oh yes, I wouldn't get rid of that for anything - my only heirloom. I hired a small storage unit in Plymouth for it, and I had to borrow a trailer from the garage to get it there and find helpers to shift it. It was quite an operation. Even getting it out of the flat was a major undertaking. It was my great-grandfather's and it's probably the only valuable thing we ever had at home. Heather used to say she was sure it was stolen, because how could a farm labourer have afforded an elaborate thing like that? And it's huge, must have taken up half the floorspace in their little cottage.'

'You should have asked us for help. I didn't realise you had to go to such lengths to find somewhere to keep it. We could have housed it until you decide where you're going to live. I would love to have it in our house for a while.'

Jamie smiled. 'But it was while you two were in Greece for two weeks and I had to clear her flat out fast, the landlord only gave me five days to do it, so I didn't have much choice, and I didn't want to pay another month's rent. Have a look.'

She got her phone out and found the photos she took at the storage facility. 'See, I got the smallest unit it would fit into, so there was just enough room for the guy at the far end to slide out without having to climb over it. Those units are narrow and deep, not very easy to work with. And here's the photo I took of it from the front before we got it into the unit, just in case the place burns down lor something. After I found out what it's worth, I insured it while it's in storage.'

'Hey, check that out, what a lovely hunk!' Gemma nodded sideways at a man who had just come in and was now talking to the barmaid, and Jamie laughed. 'Yes, lovely - but seriously Gemma, you're married to William, and you love him. And you still check out the talent wherever we go.'

'It's got nothing to do with William. Even if you have all the shoes you need, you can still admire a pair in a shop window, can't you? And don't pretend you haven't lusted after Leo Masters, even if he is your archenemy number one.'

'I know, he's attractive, but he's not my type. And what he's up to is definitely not my type of thing.' Gemma hoped she wasn't blushing, which would be embarrassing because despite being a leading force in the anti-Vista Resort protest movement, which essentially meant being anti Leo Masters, she found him devastatingly sexy. A fact never to be revealed to Gemma, who would have endless fun with the idea. Conflict of interest on a grand scale, she thought now, but it didn't change her opinion about the resort development.

'Did you see that little video clip from that film premiere, whatever it was? I can't remember the occasion because I was so busy looking at all those fabulous women and their dresses. It popped up on some news site on the Internet last week. He was there with that very tall woman with the huge eyes, you know the one, she used to be a super-model. I've seen photos of them together before, they make a great couple.'

'I didn't see it, but I think he'd get invited to everything like that, and probably she does too, if she's famous. They want beautiful people on their red carpets, gets them more publicity.'

Gemma grinned. 'And if you got invited, you'd turn it down on principle, I suppose?'

'God no! Don't be silly, of course I would go. I'd have to take a bank loan to get something glitzy enough to wear, though. No designer would lend me a dress for free advertising.'

Jamie sat in the waiting area at William's office, studying the ancient map of Devon on the wall and idly listening to the receptionist taking calls and messages. Who would have thought this little law firm would be so busy, she thought, when the girl put someone on hold while she took a message. Three solicitors in a small town and constant phone calls, how surprising!

Suddenly the girl behind the desk got to her feet and said distractedly to Jamie, who was the only person within earshot, 'Excuse me, I think I'm going to be unwell,' and disappeared down the corridor to the left. Food poisoning and early pregnancy? wondered Jamie and then the phone rang again. She hesitated for a moment and decided an unanswered phone was not good for business, so on the third ring she stepped behind the desk and picked up the phone, just as a man came in the door from the street.

'Connor & Crowther, solicitors,' she said, having

heard the greeting several times while she was waiting. 'No, I'm sorry, he's with a client. Can I take a message and ask him to call you back?'

She had no idea if the person they asked for was with a client, but taking a message seemed a good, if temporary, solution. She lifted her eyes from the note and looked at the man standing in front of her. Oh, my God, Leo Masters, just my luck.

'Good morning, you must be new,' he said. 'My name is Masters. Can you please let Jordan know I'm here?'

Jamie hesitated. She didn't know how to put a call through, or which extension was Jordan's and she didn't even know if Jordan was Connor or Crowther, or if those names still existed in the firm. Her hand hovered over the phone, while she scanned the desk for a list of extensions, but she saw nothing useful. I've left it too late, she thought, I hesitated and now he'll think I'm mad if I tell him I'm really a client. She pulled out the top desk drawer and saw nothing apart from pens and paper clips and general debris.

'Sorry - I'll go and let him know you're here.' She met his eyes and saw his impatience at her perceived incompetence; he had read the situation and decided she didn't know her job. Her cheeks burned, but before she could reply, he said curtly, 'I know the way, don't bother,' and vanished down the hallway to the right. Jamie had just returned to the client side of the desk and sat down again when the receptionist approached from the far end of the corridor and the phone rang again. The girl leaned over the desk and picked it up, talking as she walked around to her side, and William came out of his office and asked Jamie to come in. It was not until she was outside that she remembered the note she wrote, but by now the receptionist must have found it and worked it out.

It was like a comedy of errors, thought Jamie, but at least Leo Masters didn't recognise me. I should have said I don't work there, of course. I don't know why I didn't, I just got so flustered to see him right in front of me like that, he's bigger up close than he seems at a distance, and that stern face, strong and sexy at the same time. I don't normally behave like an idiot.

Walking to where she had parked her car, she smiled at the story William had told her when he handed her the letter. 'Not that I have a clue what's in it,' William had said. 'But take care where you read it. The only other time I had a letter like this to hand over, the man it was addressed to opened it in front of his wife and me – right here in this room. And then he went bright red, no, nearly purple. I thought he was going to have a heart attack. His wife tried to snatch the letter out of his hand and he lashed out and hit her quite hard and she burst into tears. Total chaos! And I never found out what was in it either – I was dying to know what got such a reaction.'

Jamie had thought she would read the letter tonight when she got home, but only two blocks away she suddenly couldn't wait a moment longer, pulled into a parking space and turned the letter over in her hands. It was a perfectly ordinary white envelope, the large squarish shape that sometimes came with greetings cards. The only writing on it was her proper name, Alexandra Jamieson. With a slight feeling of apprehension, she ripped the envelope open and pulled out two folded sheets of paper. The top one was a letter from her mother, and she read it first.

Darling Alexandra, now I can tell you who your father is (was) and why you were never told this before. In my work as a clerk at the County Court in Exeter I got to know your father, who was a barrister. I had never been married and he had been married for thirty-five years, he had four children and little grandchildren – at the time I was 42 and he was 63. We fell in love and entered into a relationship that lasted for three years until I got unexpectedly pregnant, which neither of us had even thought of. The agreement we made and signed at that time is in the envelope. Beckers, as everyone at the court called him, was a lovely, kind man with a great sense of humour, and like you he was always willing to stand up for the underdog and see justice done. I loved him dearly. With all my love, Heather

Jamie sat perfectly still for a moment and stared at the sheet of paper, before she unfolded the second sheet, which was a typed contract between Heather Jamieson and Ivor Gordon Beckwith, dated six months before her birth. It is a brief and businesslike document: Beckwith undertook to pay Heather a sum of money on the first of every month for as long as he lived 'as a contribution to 'the child's living expenses', the amount to be inflation adjusted once a year. Not 'our child', she noted wryly, just 'the child'. On Heather's part she undertook to not name him as the father, to not tell 'the child' who her father was and never contact his family. Above their signatures were three additional handwritten lines to the effect that Heather agreed to leave the area and not return, he would pay all costs involved. They had both signed it, no witnesses and that was it, short and businesslike.

Sitting in the hot car, oblivious to the world outside the windows, she tried to imagine her mother signing this; three months pregnant and in love with the man she was parting from. What had she felt? Joy at having a child from their relationship, at least? Anger at having to uproot herself and find another job? Grief at leaving 'Beckers'? And then she reneged on the promise not to tell Jamie who her father was. Did she write this as soon as 'Beckers' had died? No, she couldn't have, because her mother could not have written this concise and clear letter only a couple of years ago, when her 'pension fund' had dried up, she must have done it when she first felt her mind going. Because that's what that pension must have been, Jamie realised now, the 'maintenance' payments from Beckers. Or did the payments from Beckers continue until the estate was finalized after his death, whenever that had occurred?

So many things she would never know, and such an odd thing to have done, somehow it seemed old-fashioned, like something that might have happened in the 1940's or 1950's. He was protecting his reputation and the feelings of his family, and Heather fell in with his wishes. It was selfless love, thought Jamie, I'm so glad I found out.

She folded the sheets of paper and put them back in the envelope, shook her head and pulled out behind a delivery van, and drove back to work on autopilot.

However long ago it was since her mother wrote the letter, even after her mind started deteriorating, she had remembered to keep it. Maybe she gave it to William when she first moved to Kingsbridge, when she realised her mind was slipping away. Jamie smiled; and what could 'Beckers' have done anyway, if he'd found out that Heather had told Jamie in a letter to be handed over after her death?

She gave way to a truck with a bulldozer on the trailer coming out from the yard behind the Southwell administration building and parked in the staff parking lot.

Chapter 3

Long before her mother moved to Kingsbridge, Jamie knew that her grandparents had come from a village called Wellby on the Devon coast. Once when Jamie was a teenager, she and Heather went there for a bank holiday and stayed in a B&B in a very old cottage with oak beams in the ceilings and a picture-perfect garden. Jamie can still remember the disturbing feeling of walking along the passage to the front door on a downhill slope, small but noticeable. They took pictures of the house her mother grew up in, went into Kingsbridge for lunch one day and to Salcombe for an afternoon.

It was only when she moved to Devon herself, that she heard about the Vista Resort development and that it was going to be built right up to the border of the *South Devon Area of Outstanding Natural Beauty*, with Wellby village a stone's throw away inside the boundary of the protected area. At first this had meant little because she hadn't taken in the size and complexity of the resort, but when a protest group formed and started putting up posters, she became interested.

'Imagine this', she had said indignantly to her friend Louisa, when they talked on Skype late one night. 'This damned resort's going to cover three hundred and seventy-six acres! Hotel, cabins, heated swimming pools, a so-called water park, mini golf course, night club, bars – the lot! And their land is right bang up against where the protected area starts. And poor little old Wellby, with its cobbled streets and little cottages, ends about two hundred yards inside the boundary of the AONB. I don't know how on earth they got the go-ahead for this. For the villagers it will be like living next to Disneyland.'

'So, you've joined this protest group already – or are you just thinking of it?'

'I've joined – we can't let that Masters guy do this without making an effort to stop it. Powerful and wealthy men think they have the right to have their own way, they're so used to wield power and do what ordinary people would never get away with. They know all the right people and have access to top lawyers who can squash any objections – it's medieval, really.'

'Well, good luck!' said Louisa with a sly smile. 'I didn't realise it's Leo Masters, who owns the development company. At least you'll have something good to look at while you shout abuse at him or poke him with a stick or whatever you're planning to do – he's a very handsome beast.'

When Jamie moved to Kingsbridge, she rented the bedsit in Mrs Barnes's house because it was close to the tiny flat where Heather lived, and it was spacious and light. Mrs Barnes lived alone, and Jamie was her fourth tenant since she re-organized her house so what used to be the dining room connected to the downstairs bathroom and became a self-contained bedsit, but minus cooking facilities.

'I can't let you have a microwave oven in the room - I don't want cooking smells in the front hall,' she told Jamie, when she came to look at the room, and Jamie agreed to cook in the kitchen, after Mrs Barnes had tidied up from her own supper. And then a month after Jamie moved in, Mrs Barnes asked her to have afternoon tea with her one Sunday.

'I have a suggestion,' she said, 'and just say if it doesn't suit you, but I thought maybe we could have dinner together some days.' She looked carefully at Jamie to see her reaction. 'We get along so well, and I feel we've become friends already, so it seems a bit silly for us to cook two separate meals, one after the other.'

'That's a good idea – we've just got to work out what we both like.' Jamie smiled. 'Let's compare notes at the start and then we won't have any problems.'

The result was a very workable compromise. Jamie cooked for them two days a week, and Mrs Barnes did two days, and the rest of the time Jamie had a hurried meal at her second job at The Anchorage. There had been the odd hiccup, when Jamie was invited to have dinner with Gemma and William at short notice, but Mrs Barnes turned out to be more flexible than she seemed at the start.

Just home from work, Jamie sat in her room with a mug of tea beside her and thought ahead to the meeting of the Protect Wellby protest group that night. She had joined early the previous year and to her surprise she had become a driving force without doing anything in particular to be more than a supporter. She had a few ideas, but she knew she must be careful not to step on Brent's toes. Sometimes he seemed to want her to lead despite the fact that he had formed the group, and sometimes he resented her suggestions.

'Action, public action is what we need,' said Brent that night in the pub where they always met. He had worked for a couple of years to get some traction with the local authority, but to no avail. Part of his frustrations was probably that he knew he was ineffectual as a speaker, thought Jamie, the poor chap seemed to drift off-topic quite easily and make a muddle of his arguments. And being quite short didn't help, of course, he disappeared in a crowd. The Wellby Heritage Association had done a lot better and taken their objections further.

'Now that the Vista Resort has won the appeal and the decision stands, nobody can afford to battle against them any longer. And the ground preparation work has started in a big way, the site is crawling with men and machinery, so I suppose this is it. The Wellby heritage committee has run out of both money and pro bono lawyers. And that Wellby guy who won lots of money, the conservationist, he says he'll spend no more money on it – everyone's given up and we're the only ones left standing.'

'Maybe we could have a street march,' said Jamie. 'Invite the Wellby group, ask them to bring as many as they can get together and march up a main street, either in Kingsbridge or maybe Torquay. Just as a final gesture to mark our disapproval.'

Susan, who owned the best café in Kingsbridge instantly agreed. 'That's a great idea, but I think we should have it here, where our group is based and the closest town to Wellby. And if we have it here, there's a better chance we'll get quite a few from Wellby. Let's do it on market day and cause the first gridlock jam ever.'

'Maybe we could get media interested, get some cover nationally,' suggested Jamie, not worried about poor Brent being upset now that Susan was enthusiastic. 'We could issue a press release or contact someone in national media and use some quirky twist to get them interested. I don't know what, but I'll see if I can come up with something.'

'Good idea - let's all try to think of something that would attract attention,' said Sue and picked up her bag from the floor. 'I've got to run, email or text me if you want some help.'

The meeting broke up after a seemingly endless

discussion about days and dates, time of day and other details for the march, and they all left with a task to work on. Jamie was relieved it was over because despite the best intentions of the group, the meetings often bored her, brisk and acerbic Sue was the only exception.

Back from the pub Jamie kicked her shoes off and re-read her mother's letter for the third time, turned on her laptop and did a search for Ivor Beckwith. She found a short article from four years earlier when he was in a veteran's golf tournament and studied to photo of him closely. Too old, she decided, gravity had changed his face and she could see no likeness to herself, but he looked good for someone so old and playing golf at nearly ninety was impressive. Her thoughts were interrupted by Gemma calling, fizzing with excitement. 'Guess what! We're going to Canada for a year!'

Jamie burst out laughing at this abrupt announcement. 'Stop, stop! What's going on? When did this happen? I never heard anything about this.'

'Well, we didn't talk about it to anyone, because we didn't want to get excited - in case it never happened. We didn't even tell our families. But William applied ages ago for a scholarship to do his master's degree at the university of Toronto – it's the top one in Canada, at least the law school is, and he's just heard today that he got it! We leave in four weeks. So much to do – paperwork and stuff, packing, changing our house insurance so we can let the house, all sorts of things.'

'Oh, I'll miss you so much! I hope you do come back and don't end up staying there.'

'We can't stay, the visa is just for the duration of his studies and the firm here sponsored his application and will keep his position open. They've been really great about it. William says it's a merit point on his way to being made a partner, when Mr Crowther retires in a couple of years. I'll have to resign from the school, but maybe they'll have me back next year.'

'What about the house? I hope you get good tenants now that you've just finished doing it up. You can't have little kids running around with jammy fingers. You hear horrible stories of tenants not looking after things.'

'We've already got a tenant, an instant tenant. It's incredible how fast things are happening.' Gemma sounded as if she couldn't quite believe it herself. 'Mr Crowther's son-in-law has a job here for at least a year, he's a working on the Vista Resort project and he hasn't been able to find something his wife likes. She's a bit of a princess, I think, and they've been staying with the Crowther's, but our house got the tick of approval. She'd seen an ad for a sumptuous apartment in Salcombe, and she was holding out for that, but he convinced her they should rent our house. They'll pay market rates, and they don't have little kids with jam on their fingers.'

Jamie stayed curled up in the lovely big armchair in her room and thought of her own life, how different it would be living here now that her mother was dead, and Gemma was going away. I could move back to Bristol, go back to university full-time, or get a better job and study part-time, I've only got one year left and I'm finished. And then I won't have to deal with that creep Bridgeman and the way he always rests his hand on the back of my chair, so I can feel it against my back, I know he does it on purpose. I could re-connect with my old friends and have a life of my own again and Louisa would put me up until I found somewhere to live.

But she felt it was important to see the Vista protest through to the ultimate end. Deserting the cause now would feel like a personal defeat, and it was just about over. She picked up her book, but her thoughts reverted to the scene in the lawyer's office the other day. It was the first time she had seen Leo Masters close-up, apart from one time in The Anchorage, but then he was sitting down, and she hadn't quite realised how big he was. She wondered if he used his size to intimidate people, but surely a man like that would use every trick in the book to get his own way and come out on top, or how else had he got so wealthy at his age? Could you do it just by being smart?

'Must be at least eighty,' said Brent two days later and scanned the crowd gathered in the car park. 'The folks from Wellby are doing us proud – this is a far better turnout than I expected.'

Jamie rested her placard on the ground and regretted using the heavy piece of wood she had found in a skip. 'I don't know how I'm going to carry this monster all the way,' she said to Brent and looked at his lightweight piece of Coreflute mounted on a broom handle. 'I'll swap with you when I can't hold it up any longer.'

She tried to avoid looking at the man on the edge of the crowd, who hadn't taken his eyes off her since she first noticed him ten minutes earlier. Don't be paranoid, she told herself, he's just some guy you haven't seen before and he's come along to support the march, relax! She turned away to greet Susan who had just turned up, grateful to be diverted.

It wasn't until they were halfway down the main street that the trouble started. From around a corner came a line of men walking abreast right across the street, with very little space between them. Stretched all the way from left to right they held a long banner in front of their bodies with "We need jobs – Viva Vista!" in large black letters. Cars were backing up behind them, some drivers honked their horns, and pedestrians stopped to watch.

Taken by surprise the Vista protesters came to an untidy halt, but their opponents continued forward until the men behind the banner were pushing the group backwards. Jamie cannoned into someone behind her, there was nowhere to go and she was caught in the middle. The man right in front of her let the banner go with one hand and reached out as if to touch her face and smiled. It was the man from the parking lot, the one who had stared at her, and he wasn't a supporter, he was the opposition. The men pushed forward faster than the crowd behind Jamie could retreat and she was getting scared. She felt the crush of bodies from in front and behind, and the man opposite her smiled straight into her eyes and shouted over the chanting of the men, 'Give up, darling! You're too pretty to waste on this rubbish. You and I could have more fun on our own,' and made an obscene gesture. He was so close she felt spittle on her face and turned away sickened.

And then suddenly the men dispersed, spread out to the sides and disappeared in different directions. Only one stayed a moment longer, bundled up the long banner and ran off with half of it dragging behind him. Jamie stood confused, tried to get her heartbeat back to normal and realised that a police officer had intervened.

They completed their march, but the positive spirit from the parking lot was gone and when they were back where they had set out from, people simply melted away. Instead of staying to discuss what happened in the main street, they just walked off and left the small group of core activists, who had organized the march.

'Fucking bullies,' shouted Brent furiously and threw his placard on the ground. His face was red, and he looked as if he was on the verge of tears. 'That's riot squad tactics, that is - confronting us like that and pushing us back. Typical rednecks, they have no tolerance for other people's ideals.'

Jamie said a low-key goodbye, took a good grip halfway down the length of the wooden pole of her placard and walked away towards her car. All she wanted now was to get home to the big armchair in her room and regain her composure. She knew this reaction well and it had nothing to do with actually being hurt or in danger, it was a reflex reaction when she felt physically intimidated or the target of verbal aggression, and it would pass. But the response activated in her mind and body was not rational and reasoning would not dispel it, only time and quiet could do that. Only when she was driving away did it occur to her to wonder if the counter march was set up by Leo Masters.

Chapter 4

Friday and Saturday nights were always busy at The Anchorage; the combination of being the best restaurant in town and having the classiest bar made it very popular. Jamie's three shifts a week had enabled her to provide extras for her mother, but now she contemplated giving up the single shift she did in the bar on a Thursday night and just keeping two shifts in the restaurant. The bar work was her least favourite with too many male eyes on her, and it was too easy for men's bodies to accidentally-on-purpose brush up against hers with the occasional outright groping, when she had to come out from behind the bar.

On Saturday night Jamie put her bag in her little locker in the back room, tidied her hair in front of the mirror and walked down the passage beside the kitchen. She reported to Daniel, who had been on as front of house manager since before lunch and listened to his hand-over: one cancellation, so a table for four was available, a party of eight boisterous young men, who came in early for what might be a stag dinner to keep an eye on. And news about the second wine waiter, who had broken his finger playing squash, and had been off for two weeks but would be back the following week.

When Daniel left, she took his place behind the tall desk just inside the double doors from the foyer and smiled at two couples who entered in a flurry of wind.

'A foretaste of an early autumn perhaps,' said one of the women and ran her hands over her hair, and Jamie's evening started the way it always did with a flow of arrivals, soon followed by the earliest diners leaving. Glancing diagonally across the foyer she could see that the bar was busy, and every now and then a burst of laughter came from that direction. In a quiet moment she did a tour of the L-shaped dining room, checked that tables were serviced as they should be, asked the occasional guest if everything was satisfactory and all the while keeping an eye out for anyone coming in from the street.

She had just taken a couple of steps to one side in the angle of the L-shape to where she could see the doors in a mirror-clad pillar, when she got the feeling that someone was watching her. Leo Masters again! He was facing her from a table with a group of five others, and as soon as she met his eyes, she saw that he recognised her. His party must have come in early, before she took over. He looked at her for a long moment, she got a fleeting impression that he was puzzled, then he turned to listen to the woman on his right.

He knew her, thought Jamie, and he thought she worked at the lawyers and moonlighted in the restaurant at night. It would be quite funny if he told that Jordan guy he went to see in the law office, that he saw me here. She took the story further in her mind and smiled. And Jordan would say, 'Redhead? We've had the same receptionist for a couple of years and she's blond. Who can you be talking about?' And then they would try to work it out, and the only thing that might resolve the mystery would be if Jordan asked the real receptionist, and she remembered the note written by someone else. Another act in the comedy of errors, thought Jamie as she walked back to the desk.

Leo Masters listened with half an ear to his friend Tony's wife, Clare, telling him a convoluted story about a friend of a friend's surgery, someone he had never met. She always talked about people he didn't know and he never knew how to respond, so limited himself to the occasional 'really' and hoped for the best. Luckily, she needed little feedback and was happy to continue seemingly endlessly. Why did he feel he knew that woman with the stunning hair? He had the same feeling when he saw her at the lawyer's office the other day, straight away he felt he knew her from somewhere. But he had seen her twice now, once with her hair hanging lose, and with it up in a topknot like tonight, and he still couldn't recall ever seeing that mass of red hair and that white skin before. It was not something one would easily forget, but there was something familiar about her. Suddenly Leo realised that Clare was waiting for an answer to a question he hadn't listened to and was only saved by the waiter delivering her main course and asking if she would like her water glass topped up.

Throughout the evening, Jamie was aware of Leo Master's gaze focused on her now and then. She avoided meeting his eyes and told herself off for even caring if she did or not, because she wasn't likely to ever speak to him again. But so unsettled was she, that when she noticed that the group with Leo Masters looked ready to leave, she beckoned the wine waiter over and asked him to man the desk. You're a coward, she told her reflection in the mirror in the staff room, but she really didn't want to talk to him again. And God knows, she might make some mistake and get that impatient look from him again, and she could think of nothing worse.

Chapter 5

When Brent called and asked if Jamie has seen the notice in the local paper, she had no idea what he was talking about. 'A notice about what?'

She heard the paper rustling as he opened it to the right page, 'A public meeting about the Vista development – don't you get the paper?'

'No, I just read news online and listen to gossip in the supermarket,' she said flippantly, and Brent took it seriously, as he always did. 'That's not a good way of getting the proper news, you'll hear all kinds of rubbish! But check the Wellby Heritage Facebook page – they've just poste it.'

She found it straight away: *An invitation from Leo Masters, CEO of LM Holdings to a public meeting in the Wellby School Hall on Tuesday at 6.45 pm to discuss issues surrounding the Vista Resort development. All interested parties are welcome, no placards or banners inside, please.*

'Do you want a ride?' texted Susan, who lived in

Frogmore and came past Mrs Barnes's house on her way, and Brent called and offered to pick her up, but Jamie knew from experience that the after-match drinks session would turn into a long repetition of everything that was said, what should have been said but wasn't, and what they might say another time. She declined their offers. It's like water torture, she thought, and I'd much rather be at home reading a book or watching a movie.

On Tuesday night she arrived five minutes before the stated time and the school parking lot was nearly full, but she found a space just big enough to reverse into beside the side of the building. The hall was full to overflowing and she stood to one side of the door trying to spot someone she knew. After a moment Brent, who was at the very front, turned and waved.

'I was hoping to catch sight of you,' he said when she had made her way to the front. 'You're so good at summarizing facts, and I always get my tongue in a tangle. I'll rely on you to ask the clever questions.'

Sitting quietly on the chair Brent had kept for her, Jamie mentally listed the points she would like to make, while around her people settled into seats and talked quietly. She turned and scanned the rows of chairs behind her and recognised a few faces from the Wellby group, and towards the back a group of men she hadn't seen before. She frowned as she remembered the line of men relentlessly approaching to confront them at the street march, but she didn't recognise anyone. Turning back to the stage she tried to concentrate on what Brent was saying.

Leo Masters walked decisively from the side of the low stage to the lectern and stood there without speaking or moving until people noticed him and gradually stopped talking. No tapping on the microphone for Mr Masters, thought Jamie, reluctantly admiring his tactics. He simply relied on his presence eventually being noticed and waited, very smart. Now he had taken the upper hand without apparently doing anything, he was the top dog, and the audience were responding to his cues. She was beginning to see why he was so successful.

After three quarters of an hour the same things had been repeated many times by different people, Leo Masters had replied with the same statements slightly differently worded, and tempers in the hall were rising. Susan got to her feet on the far side of Brent and turned sideways so people behind her could see and hear. 'Mr Masters, is it true that your company made a large donation to the Historical Heritage Trust?'

'Yes.'

'And you had never made this public until you were asked yesterday?'

'No.'

'Would you have made it public, if a reporter yesterday had not shown you proof of that donation?'

Leo's face was calm, but his anger somehow emerged loud and clear. 'Are you calling me corrupt? Before you do, let me tell you that I have donated to them for many years and it's got nothing ...'

Jamie had been waiting for an opportunity at the end of the meeting. Having her say last was her tactic tonight, but now she saw that if she didn't do it soon, she wouldn't be able to do it at all. The meeting was just about to either erupt or be abruptly ended.

She raised her arm and waved it above her head, interrupting Leo Masters, who stopped talking and pointed to her. 'Yes?'

He showed no sign of recognition because with her cap on and all her hair concealed, she was far less recognizable, and once again she thought what a good idea it had been to start the habit of hiding her hair when she did things with the group. To start with she only did it to keep her identity a bit private, because her hair made her so easy to spot. But now Leo Masters wouldn't connect her with the woman who had mismanaged his appointment in the lawyer's office, which would have been so embarrassing in this context.

'Mr Masters, I would like to state my personal concerns, not those of any particular faction, but because I have historical family links to Wellby,' she said very loudly, turning half sideways like Sue had. 'Though Wellby has no Historic Places status and is not protected, apart from by being inside the South Devon Area of Outstanding Natural Beauty, it is a place of local significance. It's not just that Wellby is a pretty and homogenous village, it also has history, like the famous event when three women saved fourteen shipwrecked sailors in rowboats in a terrible storm in 1842, and the cottage where the world-renowned chemist Harold

Woodward was born in 1906. Those things are interesting and important, at least to the locals. And there are those who believe that the famous well is a source of healing, but I will leave to one side. But to find that all houses and land right up to the AONB boundary have been acquired, slowly and deliberately by you personally for years and then on-sold to your company, has naturally caused anger. They call it stealth acquisition.'

Voices were raised behind her, and she turned further and spoke louder, suppressing the feeling of intimidation caused by the raucous comments from the back of the hall. 'Can I please finish? Just give me a moment longer, please!' Despite some loud voices still calling out, she continued, speaking slowly but not much louder, to make herself heard. 'The effect of the development will be the same as building a power station next to a small cottage – incongruous and intrusive. It's only about two hundred meters from the edge of the Vista Resort land to the village, which as we all know is only just inside the South Devon protected area. The lives of those who live there will be changed forever.'

She sat down and Leo waited for the background noise to die down. 'I acknowledge all your points, and your right to feel aggrieved, but all avenues have been explored, the high court and the HPT have cleared it and the consent has been upheld. The village will still be there and...'

An angry voice from the back of the hall shouted, 'And did you make a nice personal profit by selling that land to the company?' and a man just behind Jamie raised his voice to make himself heard over the hubbub that had erupted, 'I bet you know the right people so you can get the planning rules bent.'

Leo Masters was now openly furious. 'Shut up and listen! Insulting me changes nothing. All the documentation is available for anyone to read on our company website, and there has *never* been an attempt to sway anyone in power. And don't forget the huge employment opportunities we are creating, both during the construction and ongoing - and this in an area that really needs more permanent jobs. Apart from that, Vista will bring a lot of money to the region's businesses in general, just by the increased flow of people on this side of the estuary.'

But the end of his reply was lost in a flurry of activity originating at the rear corner of the hall. Men got to their feet and took up a chant 'we want jobs, we want jobs', chairs were pushed aside as others stood up and shouted at them to leave. Within minutes the meeting turned into chaos with shouting, people pushing through the melee to get out, and men confronting each other; violence is a breath way. Then a folding chair was thrown and landed just in front of Jamie, she jumped to her feet and stood indecisive, trying to decide on a safe way out and somebody shouted, 'Watch out!'

From behind something heavy thumped into her upper back, she fell forward and hit her head on the edge of the stage. Brent dived down beside her and helped her crawl to one side, someone opened the emergency exit to the left of the stage and they got up and ran for it.

'Christ!' said Brent when they stopped a few steps from the exit among a dozen people who stared in through the open door at what looked like a brawl developing.

'That was nasty. Let me see, how bad is it?'

Blood was running down her face and her neck from somewhere above her eye, despite the protection of her cap. She wiped her eye clear with the back of her hand and clamped it over the cut on her forehead, blood trickled between her fingers and down her wrist.

'Get in my car and I'll drive you home,' shouted Brent over the noise from inside, but all Jamie wanted was to be alone, away from here. She shook her head and tried to smile, brushed his offered hand aside and headed towards her car with her hand still pressed against her forehead. People stared as she walked past them, but nobody interfered. She fumbled to unlock the car, got in and took a deep breath to steady herself before pressing the central locking button. Slowly she maneuvered through the agitated crowd with one hand on the steering-wheel and the other pressed against the wound, blinking at the sticky feeling of blood on her eyelashes.

Gemma called very early the next morning. 'God, Jamie – are you OK? Do you need some help? How bad is it?'

Sleepily Jamie tried to put these questions in context. 'What? What's the time?'

'Twenty-five past six. I saw your picture on Facebook

and Insta - it looks terrible. How badly hurt are you? How many stitches have you got?'

Instead of replying Jamie asked, 'What on earth are you doing up at half past six?'

'Oh, for heaven' sake, Jamie, it doesn't matter what I'm doing! I'm packing actually, but I need to know you're OK. You're not concussed, are you? You sound very odd.'

Jamie laughed. 'Of course not, there's no need to panic. I'm just a bit slow waking up. I fell when a fight broke out in the hall, something hit me in the back, and I crashed down without being able to catch myself. I hit my head against something, maybe the steps up to the stage, but I think my cap protected me from real damage. I've got a cut on my forehead, but it's not serious. And I don't have any stitches, I just went home and stuck some of those wound strips all over it.'

'You poor thing! Let me know if you need any help, you might well be concussed. I bet the photo will be in the national papers – all that blood - and you'll be famous, and the Vista protest will get lots of publicity. And don't forget dinner at our place tomorrow!'

Jamie checked the Internet and soon found the photo that alerted Gemma and was slightly shocked at how dramatic it was. There she was, standing by the door of her car with a wide streak of blood running down the side of her face and neck, soaking her sweatshirt, her face pale and her eyes wide. Amazing how you bleed when you cut your head, she thought and went to check her face in the bathroom mirror. This morning a swollen purplish bruise had formed around the three strips of wound tape she had used to close the cut. She gently touched the wound and flinched at how sore it was, turned the shower on and got in alongside the bloodied sweatshirt and the cap that she threw in and doused with cold water when she got home.

Chapter 6

When Jamie arrived at work the office manager instantly noticed the wound on her forehead. 'What on earth happened to you? That looks painful!'

'I tripped and fell, hit my head really hard against the edge of a … step.' Jamie sat down at her desk and wondered if Anne noticed her hesitation.

Since her first couple of months here she had known that Jack Bridgeman was aiming for the huge landscaping contract at the Vista Resort and that it was worth a fortune. The office staff followed the progress of the development and commented on the continuing protests, mostly derisively. It was only when Bridget, who processed the wages, made a vicious remark one morning, that Jamie realised her position as a member of the protest group could put her job in jeopardy.

'If every employer sacked any activists who work for them, it would soon stop,' Bridget said with cheerful nastiness. 'Those people are just delaying things when work is about to start and the whole region will have jobs for years to come. I bet Mr Bridgeman would get rid of anyone like that quick smart!'

The weekend after this conversation Jamie tied up her hair on top of her head and spent half an hour trying on caps until she found one with a high enough crown to fit over the mass of her hair. The one she bought had a fairly short peak, which didn't do much to conceal her face, but she felt that without her hair being visible nobody would recognise her at a glance. She added another item of camouflage to her activist persona when it got cold at the beginning of winter and bought a red knitted hat of the kind that sticks up above the top of your head. Perfect, she thought every time she put it on and pulled it down over her ears, I'm just an anonymous face in a crowd now.

Having dinner with Gemma and William was always fun, but this time it wasn't the casual 'come along for a meal' that they usually had. When she asked what she could bring, Gemma said firmly, 'Nothing, thank you. We want to enjoy the evening ourselves and it's quite a crowd, so we're getting food delivered. All I'll have to do is keep things hot or reheat them and put them on the table. And my mum's providing lots of pre-dinner nibbles – she can't come, but she's doing it anyway.'

Jamie dressed in her favourite aubergine dress and the silver high heels she hadn't worn for over a year and arrived to find a large group having drinks in the garden at the back, half of them unfamiliar. Probably Williams's best clients or something, she thought and stood for a moment looking out from the French doors to the terrace.

Gemma saw her and called out, 'Listen everyone, I've got to go back to the kitchen,

but here's a group introduction for those of you who don't know her. This is my lovely friend Jamie – she's knocked her head as you can see, but she's otherwise undamaged and close to perfect. You can all introduce yourselves.'

The group of six standing on the terrace just outside the doors moved apart to include her in their rather tedious debate about the redesigned traffic flow in Exeter.

'Total design fail!' said a tall, skinny man with a moustache. 'Traffic backs up further than it ever did before. I sat through two cycles of light changes the other morning.'

Jamie listened for a few minutes, decided she had nothing to contribute to the discussion and was just about to move down the stone steps to the lawn, when the blond woman beside she skinny man rolled her eyes and smiled at her.

'I'm Prissy! Hi! Why don't you and I move over a bit and get away from this endless moaning about the traffic lights. Once he starts, he's hard to stop. At home I can stuff a sock in his mouth, but I didn't bring one with me.'

They stopped slightly to one side and another woman from the group joined them. 'I'm Harriet, this crazy woman's only friend.' She held out her hand. 'I can see an amazing bruise under your hair – must be what

Gemma was talking about. Did you run into a lamp post?'

'Don't be silly, she's the one who was in the paper,' said Prissy. 'Surely you saw the photo, it looked ghastly, blood everywhere! I recognised her straight away because of her mouth.'

Both women now looked closely at Jamie's mouth, and she felt like an exhibit, but then she started to laugh. This had a slightly mad feel to it, and she said, 'I didn't know that photo had been in the paper, but I saw it on social media and it looked worse than it was.'

Ignoring Jamie's comment and continuing to stare at her mouth, Harriet said, 'Prissy, would you please explain about the mouth?'

Prissy pulled a phone from the pocket of her wide legged trousers and started tapping away while she talked. 'A perfect copy of Eva Mendes' mouth – lovely Cupid's bow, full bottom lip. Have a look at this.' She held her phone out.

'Ah, yes, now I get it. Quite un-English, very sexy.'

Jamie smiled, but she was embarrassed at the same time. 'Would you stop it, both of you! You're making me feel like some kind of freak. It's just a mouth.'

But the other two were now looking down at Prissy's phone and then up at Jamie, comparing her to someone else and it was a relief when Gemma rescued her and dragged her away to meet another couple and a man sitting at the table at the far end of the terrace.

I hope to God, she hasn't invited him as some kind of date for me, thought Jamie after a few minutes' conversation. He's totally up himself, thinks he's the global authority on everything. But to her relief the pontificating man's wife arrived just before they started the buffet meal and turned out to be someone Jamie could easily become friends with. They sat beside each other on the terrace steps with plates on their knees and had an interesting conversation about why so many books are disappointing when made into films.

'See the film first and then read the book and have a pleasant surprise,' said Jamie's companion. 'That works for me, I've done it lots of times.'

'I take the drastic route.' Jamie made a mock stern face. 'If I really love a book, I refuse to see the film however many people tell me I mustn't miss it. I just ignore it and retain my original impression of the book. No director's going to mess with my good memories.'

When her new friend went to talk to someone on the lawn, Jamie took their plates inside and found Gemma in the kitchen, leaning against the bench with a glass of wine in her hand, looking pensive. 'Why are you in here on your own? Is something wrong?'

'I'm writing a list in my head – it's what I do now. I keep thinking of stuff I must do or put in storage or pack, it never ends. What was that intense conversation that made you laugh out there before dinner? You know, when I dragged you away. I looked out from the kitchen, and I saw Prissy and Harriet looking at a phone.'

Jamie was self-conscious but tried to sound casual. 'Discussing my mouth, would you believe? They are quite mad, those two.'

'Friends from childhood, always together and quite mad, as you say. How typical of them to discuss your luscious mouth in front of you. They're kind of halfway between my mum's age and mine, and they know absolutely everyone around here. Give them another couple of glasses of wine and they'll shock the socks off you.'

Jamie drove home at midnight and thought about the discussion about her mouth and how strange it had been to be the object of such intense attention. If they were men, it would have had a sexual innuendo component, and she would have felt so uncomfortable –but those two entertaining women were just saying whatever came into their heads. It had made her laugh, even though she cringed at the same time. She had never met adults quite like them; who behaved like children and just said what they felt like without a thought for the consequences.

The night was warm and clear, but there was rain due in the next few days. She found a place to park nearly directly outside Mrs Barnes's house and stood for a moment looking up at the flawless night sky, thinking how unusual a mid-week dinner party was, and how lucky Gemma was that the rain didn't arrive early and the evening was warm. She wondered if there would be time in Gemma's busy schedule for an evening with just the two of them and suspected not. Living here when Gemma had gone would be very different, she thought. I'm not that good at making new friends, and until now

I've mostly devoted my time to Mum and work and the Vista group, and Gemma, of course.

On Saturday morning Jamie slept late after a busy Friday night at The Anchorage. She lay in bed listening to the distant sound of the radio, the background noise that was always on in Mrs Barnes's kitchen and thought what a blessing a comfortable bed was. She had slept like a log ever since she moved into this room. Her phone buzzed, and she reached lazily for it: an email from Southwell's. Abruptly she sat up with a feeling of apprehension; the only time she had emails from work was when the system automatically emailed her pay details.

'Two minutes ago, I was happy,' she said out loud when she had read it, 'and now I'm furious - and worried.' She read the short message again.

"Your employment has been terminated with immediate effect as it has come to our notice that you have publicly acted contrary to the best interests of the company. Your remaining pay will be credited to your bank account on Monday along with any accumulated holiday entitlement. If you have any personal belongings in our office, please advise and we will forward them to your address. J.S. Bridgeman."

She got out of bed, pulled the curtains back and opened the window on a cool, cloudy morning that perfectly suited her mood. She thought back to the lectures about employment law and felt nearly certain that Bridgeman couldn't legally do this, but she must read her contract and check the details. It must be that photo in the papers, he had discovered she belonged to the protest group, but was that enough reason for him to sack her; something she did in her own time without any connection to her job?

I'm nominally a temporary employee, she thought, even though I've been there for so long. Does that affect my rights?

She showered with her mind in turmoil, alternating between anger at the brusque dismissal and worry about finding a new job in an area where not much was likely to be available at the end of the summer season. In the end she called Gemma, though she knew it was unfair to ask for help when they were practically ready to leave the country.

'That bastard!' exclaimed Gemma. 'He's got a dreadful reputation and he drinks too much. He's been in trouble over his behaviour in bars a couple of times. William's police mate at the Plymouth station told him Bridgeman nearly got prosecuted for sexual assault a couple of years ago, when he did something utterly unspeakable in a night club there. It was only because the waitress didn't want to give evidence in court that he got away with it – and she was probably scared he'd get the owner to sack her. I think I remember William saying he's done that before. Hang on and I'll get him for you.'

William listened to the story and what her opinion was, asked her to email her contract, if she had an electronic copy and promised to read it right away. She sent the contract and only had time to get dressed and brush her teeth before he called back.

'I think you're right about this,' he said regretfully. 'It

would need to go to the Employment Tribunal and that can take a while, so it's probably better to write it off as a loss and get another job. I'm sure he'd use that clause you pointed out to claim he has the right to fire you - that standard para about not engaging in any activity likely to bring you employer into disrepute or cause him loss of business. But he could also use the fact that the contract is eighteen months old and was supposed to be for three months - *you* could claim it means you're now a permanent employee, but he would point out you never used your right as stated in paragraph 5.1.2 to ask for a performance review and have your employment status re-assessed. If we weren't going away, I'd love to have a go at taking this unpleasant man to the cleaners, but I can't.'

'Thanks, William, I think I'd better leave it – it sounds like a losing battle.'

She stayed there looking out over the garden for a long time, deep in thought. She knew William was right, the process would eat up time and money, and she might still not get anywhere. She might be offered either an amount of money as compensation or the original job back, if the tribunal decided that belonging to the protest group was not a genuine reason to sack her, but she'd probably only get a small amount and working for that man again was out of the question, it would be unbearable. Much better to cut her losses and look for another job. First, she would talk to the manager at The Anchorage and ask for as much relief work as they could give her when people were off sick, or maybe he could give her some extra hours in some other role. And then it was job search time again.

Saying goodbye to Gemma and William was harder than Jamie has anticipated, a real wrench of sadness, and afterwards an empty feeling, a void that she knew she couldn't fill. She hadn't realised how very close they had become, she thought, as she watched Gemma's mother drive them away. She had many other friends that she had known since school and always kept in touch with, but two were more important than any others: Louisa, who was the anchor in her life, and Gemma, who was more like a sister. She continued watching until the car was out of sight, then drove back to Mrs Barnes's house, wondering what she should do now.

MY ENEMY, MY LOVE

Chapter 7

Leo came across the photo of Jamie during a morning trawl through the on-line news and his hand with a spoon of cereal remained suspended halfway to his mouth while he scanned the text, which described the chaotic meeting. The image was startling, a young woman with blood obscuring nearly half her face, smudged where she has roughly wiped it out of her eye. She stood beside a car with one hand on the open door and the other clutched to her forehead, eyes wide open and looking straight at the camera; her pale sweatshirt wet with blood.

Shit! he thought, appalled at the sight. I didn't realise she'd been so badly hurt - or hurt at all. I saw her fall and her friend got her out the side door, but I never got a look at her face. Those morons who created the mayhem – they say they want jobs, and fair enough, but throwing chairs at people who have a different opinion, crazy. I think that's what hit her, the second chair. Bet she's got a bruise on her back. If I knew where to find her, I'd call and ask how she is, send her some flowers to cheer her up.

He found it hard to admit to himself that he was attracted to this frontline opponent to his plans, had been since the first time he noticed her. He was already strongly attracted to the redhead from the restaurant, and it felt slightly creepy that he could apparently fancy two women at the same time. Was it due to long abstinence, or was he having an early mid-life crisis? He banished the thought from his mind, he had no time to waste on his personal concerns right now; the project was finally under way, and he would be very busy for a long time, so fantasizing about women was off the agenda.

Chapter 8

Jamie knew that Jerry, who managed The Anchorage, worked on Saturdays and had Sunday and Monday off, so she texted and asked to speak to him before he left for the day, and he told her to come about four.

'Could you please keep me in mind for any relief work that crops up?' she said and wondered at the wooden expression on his face, so unlike him, a naturally gregarious man. 'Or any shifts that are become available. I've got more time on my hands now and I need to earn some more money.'

'Sorry,' he said, looking slightly to one side of her. 'I was planning to catch up with you next week to say we'll not need you for the Friday nights any longer. Stu, who's been with us longer than you, wants more hours and you're a casual, so he's taking the Friday night shift in the restaurant.'

Jamie felt sick. She knew she was miles better at the job than Stu, and Jerry had praised her for her poise and her ability to deal with demanding people on several occasions. That look on his face, she could see how uncomfortable he was, trying to look as if this was routine, but she didn't believe it. He wasn't enjoying telling her, and she wondered if Bridgeman put pressure on him. It wasn't hard to imagine that everyone in business in a small town knew everyone else and could cash in favours or exert a bit of pressure.

'Well, that's my bad luck, but I hope you'll remember me if anything becomes available.' She got up and thought, like if Stu gets run over by a truck, preferably one of Southwell's.

With nearly two hours to go before her evening shift started, she paused indecisively outside and tried to think what to do. Seriously worried about her future she walked to the bar where she and Gemma had held their two-person wake for Heather. It was still early for bar-goers, and the place was less than half-full. Slightly disappointed that the sexy barmaid was not on duty, she ordered a tonic with lemon and ice and took it to a booth in the far corner of the room. Two men standing at the end of the long bar with drinks in front of them moved down the room to sit at a table not far from Jamie's and she made a point of not looking their way.

She opened the BBC news app on her phone and scrolled through the headlines, then began reading an in-depth article about rainforest devastation and a few minutes later she sensed movement out of the corner of her eye. One of the men from the table nearby was standing beside her, and when she looked up, he smiled.

'We thought you might want to join us if you're not waiting for someone.'

He was a decent looking man in his forties, but she needed time to herself, and she wasn't in the mood for a conversation with strangers.

'I'm waiting for my brother,' she said, a response she had made up years ago and had used many times since. 'He won't be long, but thanks for asking.'

She continued to read undisturbed, oblivious of the increasing number of people around her. Now and then she checked the time and at quarter to seven she left to go back to The Anchorage. A man at the bar, who had observed her steadily in the mirror behind the line-up of bottles, swivelled on his stool, watched her pass through the door and smiled to himself.

Chapter 9

There was no delaying it, and Jamie knew the old lady would be upset. They got along so well, and it was only a few weeks since Mrs Barnes told her that she was the nicest tenant she could ever have wished for.

She found her landlady sitting on the terrace outside the living room with a cup of tea and Jamie took the chair beside her.

'I'm very sorry, Mrs Barnes, but I have to leave my lovely room here. You know I lost my full-time job, and now I've lost one of my shifts at the restaurant too. I just can't afford to keep the room. I have to find something smaller and cheaper.'

'Oh, no – please don't leave!' Mrs Barnes's chubby face screwed up in distressed creases. 'We get along so well, and you are such a good tenant. And we are so used to each other, too. And I love having someone to share dinner with. I could lower the rent a bit and then you could stay, or maybe you could stop paying rent until you find a new job.' She pushed the plate of biscuits towards Jamie. 'Have a biscuit, dear – they're a new kind I saw in the supermarket yesterday.'

Jamie took one and tried to divert Mrs Barnes from her various schemes to make it possible for her to stay, but she was forced to leave the issue hanging. Mrs. Barnes seemed unable to accept Jamie's decision as a fact, and after sitting with her for half an hour, Jamie left her there and returned to her room.

She knew very well that Mrs. Barnes's suggestions were not practical, and the problem would be solved when her middle-aged son found out. Mrs Barnes told him everything on his two-weekly visits from Taunton, and he would forbid it. He guarded her interests as if they were his own, which he was surely hoping they would be one day in the not too distant future. That was nasty, thought Jamie, but he was an unpleasant man and he a had never forgotten that she had turned down a date with him when she first moved in.

It took nearly a week to find something she could afford on what she earned at The Anchorage now, but she had to assume that she might not find a job for a couple of months or maybe longer, and her savings must be made to last. The day she left her room with the chintz-upholstered armchair and the lovely queen-size bed, she hugged Mrs Barnes and felt as if she was orphaned all over again.

. . .

After too many trips to count she had finally carried all her belongings down the narrow lane and up the steep iron stairs on the outside of the building to her new room. The room could be accessed from inside the welding factory; it was on a mezzanine floor next to the office, but the place was locked up at night and the number of steps was the same inside and out. She wiped her damp face with her sleeve and told herself it was good to start out as she meant to continue.

'It used to be a second office and the bathroom was just an extra, nobody ever used it, and we don't need two offices,' said the man who had showed her the room and looked around as if he wasn't displeased with what he saw. 'It's not too bad, is it? Hasn't been used for a while, but you'll soon air it out.'

The rent was so low she couldn't afford not to take it, but it was ghastly and she had never lived anywhere so depressing and so shabby. All there was in this dingy beige room was a single bed, a chest of drawers that smelled of mouse droppings, two wooden chairs and a small table. Her cartons ended up stacked three high along the wall and she used them to put things on; there was no shelf and no wardrobe, so she couldn't unpack them. She would just have to put the summer clothes away in the boxes and get warmer clothes out later, or maybe she should have done that to start with. It was autumn now and the weather could change at any time.

She went out and bought what she needed in the way of cleaning materials and spent the afternoon scrubbing the toilet and handbasin to remove what looked like years of grime, she cleaned the window and washed the floor. She gave up on the shower and decided that the dirt in the corners wouldn't come out and stick to her, so she'd try to ignore it.

The first night in the room she hardly slept at all, her mind constantly reverted to thoughts of how to salvage her life from this pit of disasters, and how to get back to normal without spending all her reserves if she couldn't find a job soon.

In the morning she woke hungry and exhausted and tried to plan her new existence. Living on cheap take-away food was not an option, and she had no way of cooking. The chef at the restaurant would give her something to eat in the kitchen at the end of her shift, but staff weren't allowed to take food home. Reluctantly she decided she must spend some of her carefully monitored savings on a cheap microwave oven, so she could make coffee and heat simple meals. She would check the notice board in the supermarket, where there always seemed to be household things for sale in amongst the notices about bikes and cars.

It seemed incredible that she had ended up like this. And why didn't she see it coming? she wondered when she showered in the uninviting bathroom. Only a couple of years ago, she had been a top student with a nearly completed law degree, a good part-time job that paid well, and a nice room in a small, terraced house she shared with a couple of really nice girls. Since moving to Kingsbridge one thing after another has eroded all the precious confidence she managed to build up after she left

Douglas, and now she was adrift, at the mercy of circumstances and the actions of others.

She hadn't told Gemma what happened, because she couldn't bear the thought of Gemma being worried about her when she was so far away and couldn't help. Gemma would offer her a room in their house if they weren't in Canada, but now was not the time to tell her. When she had found another job and could move out of this dismal room, she would make a good story out of it and Gemma would exclaim, 'You should have told me!'.

The brief temptation to call Louisa and ask her for advice or help was squashed before it became irresistible. Louisa was many years older than Jamie and a firm rock in her existence, but she had already spent endless time and effort restoring Jamie's confidence and motivation after Douglas. She couldn't ask her again, not that she wouldn't do it, but Jamie felt that she should now be able to cope on her own. And anyway, this wasn't total a disaster, it was just a setback. She would only tell Louisa about this room later on, when she was in a better place or she would feel she must do something about it.

Chapter 10

Jamie put the address in the Navigate app on her phone and set out to pick up a microwave she had found a notice for on the board at the supermarket, one that had sounded nearly too good to be true. Hawker Street turned out to be a short one-way street off Saffron Park, where she had never been before. As soon as she opened the car door, she smelled jasmine and the scent brought back memories of a flat where she had lived with her mother when she had just started school. She stopped by the garden fence, where swathes of jasmine hung like heavy draperies, inhaled and was for a moment lost in images from her childhood.

'Isn't it lovely? It's flowered all through the summer,' said a woman's voice. 'My husband gets cross, but I refuse to cut it back.'

An overweight young woman stood in the open front door with a toddler perched on one shelf-like hip. 'You must be Jamie - you'll have to come in and carry the oven out yourself,' she said cheerfully and tucked Jamie's ten-pound note into a cleavage that could conceal a small fortune. 'I can't put the kid down or he'll start screaming again and my husband's asleep – he does shiftwork.'

The microwave was waiting on the kitchen bench and Jamie looked at it in surprise. 'It looks nearly new! Are you sure ten pounds is enough?'

'Look, I just want to get rid of it,' said the woman. 'My hubby earns good money, and we bought a really big model so I can fit bigger casserole dishes in. This one works just fine – you need it and I'll be happy if someone gets it off the bench.'

Jamie carried the oven and her little supply of food up the scary iron stairs and considered where to put it. Not in the tiny bathroom because it would mean buying an extension cord and have one of the chairs in there to put it on, so it would have to sit on the cardboard box shelf. She was pleased she had got boxes all nearly the same size from the supermarket; they made a great shelf. She moved her stacks of folded clothes over to make room, puts the microwave oven on the end box nearest the wall socket and stood back. Not bad, basic but tidy, she thought, and then went back to the car to fetch the other things she had picked up in the second-hand shop. As soon as her little kitchen arrangement was unpacked, she made herself a cup of coffee to celebrate and sat on her bed, admiring what she had laid out on a towel: one mug, one glass, two plates, cutlery and a breadboard.

. . .

Waking up the next morning and being able to have a hot cup of coffee with her slice of Ryvita with peanut butter made her feel quite cheerful, as did the thought that today she was having morning tea with Mrs Barnes.

'I miss you, Jamie, even though you've only been gone a couple of days,' Mrs Barnes said yesterday when she called to invite her. 'We always had such lovely chats, you and I. And if I hadn't let my son persuade me, you would still be here, for free. As it is, the room sits empty, which I could have told him would happen at this end of the season, and I'll tell him so when he comes next weekend. I don't know why I listen to him.'

Jamie came out of the lane to the street at the back, where she had parked the car, and there was nothing to be seen apart from a van and a pick-up truck. She stared at the place where she parked it when she brought the oven back, opposite the roller door at the saddlery.

Inside the saddler's there was a lovely smell of leather and oil and the shop was full of racks and stands laden with things that Jamie had no idea what they were but found very appealing, all gleaming leather and shiny metal fastenings. Two saddles sat on a contraption that looks like a metal cage; objects of beauty made of deep brown leather with waxed thread stitching.

'Did you notice my car when you arrived this morning - the yellow VW?' she asked the man behind the counter. 'I park it in the same place every day and now it's gone. Did you see it?'

'I saw it last night when we locked up, but it wasn't there this morning. My partner stayed a lot later than I did yesterday, I'll go out the back and ask him.' He came back shaking his head. 'He left at quarter past eight, he was finishing off some work, and your car was there then.'

Jamie thanked him and was about to leave, when a young woman emerged from the back area. 'Ruben says you're asking about your car,' she said. 'The bright yellow one? Yeah, I noticed it wasn't there this morning.' She looked pityingly at Jamie. 'I was here very early, got here just after seven, lots to do just now and I thought of it not being there when I turned into our yard. It's such a cheerful colour and it brightens up this boring street – and it's been there every morning for a while now, so I reckoned it belonged to someone who lives close by.'

Jamie thanked them and stood on the pavement Googling how to report a stolen car in Kingsbridge, where there was no police station. Not that knowing when it was taken made any difference, and probably most car thefts happened at night, but there was just the tiniest chance someone had seen something.

She had just found the online form, when the man from the saddlers came out to ask if she wanted a ride to Torquay. 'I'm going there this morning to deliver a saddle, so I can give you a ride.'

He smiled grimly at her uncomprehendingly look. 'Rural Devon and Cornwall constabulary has been reduced to less than we used to have, so now the nearest actual police stations are in Torquay in one direction or Plymouth in the other. But I'm heading off to Torquay in half an hour, so if you want to come, you're welcome.'

'Thanks, but I can do it online. I've just looked it up and I can deal with the insurance claim online too. It will be a curse not having transport.'

'It is a terrible shame. I suppose you need the car to go to work,' he said, and Jamie thought of the long walk home at night after her two remaining weekly shifts at The Anchorage. And how slow the process would be to first make the insurance claim and then find a car she can afford, and how hard it will be to get to places to even look at second-hand cars. She would get a bus timetable, because she knew without looking up the paperwork, that she didn't have the kind of insurance that provided you with a replacement car while they processed the claim.

'I think I need a bike,' she said out loud, not really addressing her kind helper, but he turned out useful.

'Try Mike's Barn. It's beside his house on the road towards Wellby, you can't miss it – just outside town. Retired guy who restores and repairs all kinds of things – including bikes. I'll drop you there if you like, not much out of my way, just a different route.'

She accepted the offer of a ride and called Mrs Barnes to cancel their date for morning tea.

"Mike's barn" was a large old stone barn with wide double doors close to each corner standing open to a dimly lit interior. A man in blue overalls was bending over a workbench just inside the left-hand door and turned when he heard Jamie's footsteps on the gravel, a tall skinny man in his late sixties with thinning grey hair and a huge moustache. Thank God I'm not deaf, thought Jamie, when she got a closer look at him, nobody could lip-read this guy, you can't even see if he's got a mouth.

'Bikes,' he said slowly, as if a bike was something rare and precious that didn't often come his way. 'I do get one of those now and then. Come along and we'll see what we can find.'

He led the way down a row of lawnmowers, followed by a few rotary hoes. They turned a corner and walked along the back wall and then up another long aisle on the other side. There was machinery everywhere, most of it unfamiliar to Jamie, and in the open space in the centre of the floor, three large machines roosted like dormant giants, surrounded by parts and tools. Jamie and her companion emerged at the front right corner of the barn, where the huge doors were wide open, and Jamie realised he was teasing her. At least thirty bikes of various sizes were neatly parked alongside each other, with their front wheels angled the same way, and they could easily have walked across the front of the barn to reach them instead of right around the inside. She started to laugh and Mike's moustache changed position in a way that probably meant he was smiling.

'Oh my God, one or two! This is a treasure trove.'

'It is, and you probably wouldn't believe how many old things people bring in and how many leave here each week, fully operational again.' Briskly, he pulled half a dozen bikes out, seemingly at random, but she soon realised that he had estimated her height, and he knew what he was about. 'Try these, take them for a spin on the road and see what you think.'

Half an hour later she set out to ride back to Kingsbridge on her new, second-hand bike unexpectedly cheered by the feeling of being mobile once again. Hanging on the handlebar was an old-fashioned bike basket, thrown in for free when Mike heard that her car had been stolen.

Chapter 11

When a loud voice called out from across the frozen food counter in the supermarket, Jamie flinched with embarrassment, but all eyes were on Prissy, who was waving both arms above her head and smiling widely.

'Jamie - yohoo!' she called. 'Hang on, darling, I'm coming around to your side! How nice to see you - God, you look so thin!'Jamie waited and hoped that Harriet wasn't shopping at the same time because the two of them together in a public place like this could turn into the kind of performance she would rather not be part of. But Prissy was on her own and seemed truly delighted to bump into Jamie. She arrived with her trolley on Jamie's side of the freezers and looked her up and down.

'Please don't lose too much weight,' she said. 'This is nearly the thin edge of the wedge – get it?' She laughed, delighted with her joke. 'But seriously, darling, I shouldn't joke about it. You're not ill, are you?' She took hold of Jamie's hand, suddenly serious and genuinely concerned.

'Oh no, not at all. But my car got stolen and I bought a bike until everything with the insurance is sorted out, so I'm probably using more calories than I used to.'

Protecting her privacy felt important now, avoiding exposing her plight to people she hardly knew and see pity in their eyes. There was no way she was going to tell anyone that she was eating minimally to save money. She knew it was a false economy, but the thought of applying to the social services for assistance was the thing she feared most; the final proof that she was a complete failure. Had she known what the future would reduce her to, she might not have chosen to leave her studies and her great job in Bristol to come here to be close to Heather, she thought but suppressed the thought as unworthy.

'Let's go and have a coffee! I'd love to have a chat.' Prissy leaned over and studied Jamie's basket. 'You haven't got anything that will thaw out and drip, do you? Let's go to the Wheelhouse – it's nice down there by the water.'

Jamie allowed herself to be led to the checkout, paid for her purchases and followed Prissy out into the carpark.

'Where's your bike?'

'Right here, I'll meet you at the café, bet I'll be there before you.'

.   .   .

They sat outside under an umbrella with an iced coffee each and Jamie looked at the sun on the water and smiled. 'I can't believe it – one day it's like real autumn has arrived far too early and then we get weather like today. But they say we're going to have an early autumn, and cold. I suppose mid-September is autumn, isn't it?'

'You know what I think?' Prissy sucked whipped cream noisily through her straw. 'I think it was always like this, back and forth, unseasonal weather, uneven, but we kind of glamourize the past. We think back to summers when we were children or teenagers, and in our memories the sun always shone right through July and August and it never rained even in September.'

'You're exactly right. It's only when I think of particular events, that I remember any bad weather in the summer at all. Like the holiday when I was thirteen or fourteen and my mum took me for a holiday in Dorset, a little place near a beach. We rented a caravan someone kept in a field there, and it rained nearly the whole time. We played endless games of poker and my mom won my entire fictional fortune and left me destitute, so I had to beg for food at dinner time.'

Prissy laughed. 'My God, fancy having a mum who played poker for a fictional fortune! Mine taught me how to play bridge and how to place the cutlery correctly when you set the dinner table.'

Jamie smiled at the thought of her mother, who was anything but conventional and always willing to take a risk and hope for the best. 'She was quite old for a mother, she was forty-six when I was born, and she was a bit unusual, I suppose. She didn't really care what people thought. I remember going into a bookshop with her once, I was probably about eleven at the time and she asked the assistant to suggest some nice, sexy books – for me! I nearly died of embarrassment and the assistant was very disapproving. But she did find some and she bought them – 'you might as well learn about it in a nice fictional context' she said, or something along those lines.'

'And talking about wet holidays,' said Prissy with a naughty grin. 'Beat this one if you can, Nick and I spent our two-week honeymoon in a campervan in Scotland and it rained every single day!'

'That sounds grim – did you have a pack of cards?'And Prissy said casually, 'God no! Nick might be a persistent talker, but he a demon in bed. I think we spent most of the two weeks in the sack.'

They both burst out laughing, and the elderly couple two tables away looked disapprovingly at them, which made them laugh harder.

'We must get together again – you and me and Harriet. This was such fun!' said Prissy. 'Now that I've got your phone number, I'll be able to text you. And how come you're not at work, anyway – have you got a day off?'

'I left my job a couple of weeks ago – I didn't much like the boss. If you hear of anything, let me know!'

She walked off towards her bike before Prissy thought to ask where she used to work and what was wrong with the boss. Discretion isn't in her vocabulary, thought Jamie.

She just asks and says whatever comes into her mind. Mostly funny, but a bit cringe-making too. And who knows, maybe Bridgeman is her uncle or a connection of some kind, which would make us both feel very awkward, well, at least I would.

Chapter 12

Brent called in the evening, just when she had put her packet of noodles in a bowl of water and turned the microwave oven on.

'A few of us, the core of the group I suppose you could say, have decided to do a one-off protest at the gates to the Vista site. Like a farewell and a reminder that not everyone around here is happy, even if the development is a done deal. We haven't decided on a day yet. Will you come?'

'Of course, just tell me when and I'll be there.'

'I can pick you up from work and take you out there if you like. Sue said you're riding a bike everywhere these days, and she heard your car got stolen - it's quite a long way. But we want to be there a bit before the workers leave for the day, so we can cause a bit of a stir. I hope you can get away from work half an hour early.'

How does Sue always know these things, wondered Jamie, it's like she has a private surveillance system in place, you hardly have time to walk from the hairdresser to your car and she'll send you a text saying, 'nice haircut!'. Must be all the gossip she hears in her café.

'I'm not working at Southwell's now - they sacked me, such a bummer! And the restaurant canned one of my shifts, so I had to move, my old place was too expensive, and my income has shrunk to nearly nothing. If you hear of any work let me know.'

'That's tough, but you should have told me. Plonk and I have a third bedroom that we've never let – it's tiny, but you could have it rent free till you get a new job.'

'Thanks, Brent, it's very kind of you, but I've moved now and I'm happy where I am.'

No way! she thought when they ended the call. He had been quite keen in a hesitant way for a while and she didn't want to have free accommodation from someone who even mildly fancied her, besides which he wasn't her type at all, and she disliked the guy he shared with. She was better off in her ghastly garret, and thanked her lucky star he was so easily diverted. Having side-tracked himself he'd forgotten about wanting to give her a lift and she could avoid a final tedious after-match session in the pub.

On Thursday night Jamie rode her bike to work in the bar. Not because it was too far to walk, but she felt safer riding the bike home after work than walking. The last couple of weeks, she had seen the man from the street march several times, and she had become acutely aware of the disadvantage of not having the car.

I never thought of it before, she thought as she turned the second to last corner, but in a car you're in a bubble of safety, press the button for the central locking and you're safe. Walking you're an easy target, and the bike is at least faster than walking, bet I could out-bike a guy running.

She turned the last street corner towards the back entrance of The Anchorage, and there he was at the end of the block, the man from the street march, coming towards her. Was it coincidence? She estimated the distance between them and continued at normal speed, so she could turn into the alleyway to the back entrance before he got there. She hoped he didn't see that she noticed him, but he raised his hand in a mock salute. Leaning the bike against the wall she hurried inside, felt a need to rush, to be out of sight before he walked past. Kingsbridge was a small town, but even so she seemed to see him more often than one would expect. Or did she just notice him more than other people because he freaked her out?

The whole evening became one long period of apprehension, waiting for him turn up in the bar, to turn around and find him a meter away staring at her or to have to walk past him. None of these things happened and at the end of her shift she sat in the tiny staff locker room for three quarters of an hour, until the kitchenhand who lived further out of town along the same route as her, had finished. She asked for a ride and said she'd been bothered by a man and didn't want to ride her bike alone in the dark, and they left together. She knew the man from the street march might already know where she lived, but this was the best she could do.

Jamie woke to a cool morning with clouds scurrying across the sky in a blustery wind and decided to spend the day inside; it was Friday and she no longer had a Friday shift in the restaurant. She looked across at her cardboard box shelf and saw the two tins of soup she bought the day before, so there was no need to go out at all. But mid-afternoon, when she was deep in a book, her phone pinged with a message from Sue: *Just in case Brent forgets to txt you about transport– off to the vista site this afternoon at 4.30, do you want a ride, we're going in his car.*

Brent had forgotten to even tell her which day they had decided on, but Sue's text suited her. She replied that she didn't need a ride, hoping Sue would think she was going with someone else. But she knew the after-match function was bound to be more dire than usual after this final act, so it would be like a wake. She decided she couldn't bear it, dismantled part of the cardboard box shelf and located her ankle boots and a pair of thick socks.

Chapter 13

When Jamie arrived at the Vista site, only one member of the protest group was there, a man whose name she couldn't remember, a quiet middle-aged man who had rarely said anything in meetings.

'What a rotten start to the autumn!' She smiled and unzipped her storm jacket as she walked towards him. 'They say it's going to rain later.'

'Did you bike from Kingsbridge? I could have picked you up - it must have been a struggle in this wind.'

She pulled the red wool beanie down over her ears. 'Keeps me fit and saves money, and the wind will be behind me when I go back.'

He made no reply, just shook his head at her, and they waited in silence until Brent arrived with three others in his car. They stood on the damp grass to one side of the gates and discussed how to arrange themselves to cover the full width of the access road for best effect.

'Depends on how many turn up from Wellby,' said the

man whose name she couldn't remember. 'I called quite a few and they said they'd try to make up two or three carloads, one final fling before it's over. We should have enough to block the road two or three deep.'

Isn't it funny, thought Jamie as she listened to him, he's been to most of our meetings and other things like the street march, and he's hardly said a thing in all that time – and now, suddenly he speaks in whole sentences and provides nuggets of information, I wonder what brought this on.

By ten to five the group was much bigger than Jamie would have expected. Six cars arrived more or less in convoy and parked back where the edge of the road was wider and flatter. People greeted each other, commented on the weather and put forward theories on how the blockade would work out. Jamie waited until Sue took charge and they arranged themselves as she suggested, with Jamie, Brent and Sue together in the middle of the road, right outside the gates. A few others formed a line at both sides of them with the rest massing close behind. Jamie turned her head and smiled at Sue. 'I'm surprised so many turned up.'

'Well, one last push, as they say.' Sue pulled her collar up and buttoned the top button. 'God, it's getting cold! I suppose everyone felt like we did, this is the final event, and we might as well make it a good one.'

Within minutes of them blocking the road, two security guards appeared outside their cabin and one of them approached the gates and called out, 'You can't stand here, we've got trucks and vehicles that need to get through. Would you please move to the sides of the road?'

'We are a making a final protest against the Vista project,' said Brent loudly. 'We know we can't stop it, but we want to make sure the world knows that not everyone agrees with profit driven so-called progress changing the whole countryside.'

Jamie was quite impressed. Brent had rehearsed this statement, which was better phrased and more to the point than anything she'd heard him say in public before. The guard came out through the smaller gate on one side and Brent took a step forward until they were right up close; now the guard was getting angry.

'Right! You've made your point – and filmed it, I see, so now you can step to the sides and clear the road.'

'And what are you going to do about it?' asked Brent and his tone made the guard furious, he raised his voice. 'I'll damn well move you myself if you won't get out of the way.'

'Do it!' Brent taunted him, and the other guard came through the gate with a phone in his hand, talking as he advanced.

Jamie couldn't believe that Brent had suddenly developed such a staunch façade and thought what a pity it was that he hadn't display this kind of courage in the face of those men with the banner at the street parade. A brawl would have got a lot of media attention.

'OK, guys, move over! This has gone on long enough.' The second guard came to stand next to his colleague. 'We've got trucks that need to get out and workers wanting to go home very soon. Enough is enough!'

He put his phone back in his pocket and glanced over his shoulder as he spoke. Jamie could feel slight movements to her left and behind her, some were shifting from foot to foot, anticipating that the group would move to the sides. But before anyone broke the line, Leo Masters appeared and came through the gate. He motioned for the guards to step back and came right up to Brent, who had maintained his position out in front of the main group.

'I know that you're upset and disappointed,' said Leo, his expression was neither angry nor threatening, his stance relaxed. 'But we all know this is over now. There's nowhere to take your protest further, you can't take it through the courts again. And even if someone tried, they'd fail – it's over.'

Jamie listened to the ensuing debate between Brent and Leo Masters and thought how useless this was, it wouldn't change anything. Hopefully Brent wouldn't start anything physical, but his body language was aggressive and she had never seen him like this before. If Leo Masters hit him, Brent would be flattened, he was no match for someone so much bigger. How she wished they hadn't decided to do this; Masters was right, the battle was over.

As she listened, she was grateful that Masters at least seemed to know how to keep his temper in check, because this could go wrong in the blink of an eye. He seemed very calm and not at all aggravated, quite odd really, you'd expect him to be fed up with yet another protest at this stage.

And then, in a surprising and disarming move, Masters smiled and held his hand out. 'You've fought a good fight and done your damnedest. Let's end this without any empty gestures that won't achieve anything. Shake?'

And to Jamie's huge relief Brent's stance relaxed after a few seconds hesitation and they shook hands. Leo Masters followed the guards through the gate and the protesters slowly dispersed. Brent was visibly upset, close to frustrated tears and went straight to his car with the people who had come with him half running to catch up.

Jamie stood on the side of the road and stared at the empty space where she had left her bike leaning against a tree. She walked further in among the trees and looked around, but there was no bike to be seen. Bet it's one of those guards, she said to herself, they were much angrier than Masters, maybe a third one came out of the pedestrian gate when the other two were arguing with Brent, maybe he moved it just to annoy us.

She continued walking along the tall perimeter fence and scanned the surrounding trees as she went; further and further from the road until the fence made a dog leg turn and dark trees with larger canopies blocked the rapidly fading light. She remembered the outline of the site from the planning documents; this was where the site came up to the edge of the oak forest, and she wondered how much further the Vista fence went or if it went right around the entire site.

As the rain started falling and the sky darkened further, she tried to calculate how far it would be around the whole site and how long it would take to walk and continued stubbornly onward. When she finally gave up and started back along the fence, she had no idea why she walked so far, why common sense had not made her turn around sooner. Anyone hiding her bike would have done it far closer to the gates. Thick black clouds from horizon to horizon had made the dusk interval short and now it was nearly completely dark. In a couple of places, she triggered lights that suddenly blinded her; she turned her head to the side. Walking along the rough ground in the dark was difficult, once she tripped on an obstacle and bent her ankle painfully sideways. By the time she was back at the main gates, her shoulders were wet inside her jacket, her ankle was hurting, and the only comfort was the red wool beanie keeping her head warm.

Jamie put her hands in her pockets and started out along the road and tried to guess how long it would take to walk back to Kingsbridge. If anyone remotely decent looking offered her a ride she would accept. But the road was empty, the workers had left long ago and there were no streetlights here. As soon as she was out of the bright light at the gates, the darkness became total and only the edge of the seal guided her feet.

Chapter 14

eo leaned against the wall beside the security guard's desk and listened to his endless litany of complaints about 'those bastards' and what a nuisance they were.

'It's not just those nutters outside the gate this afternoon,' he said. 'Some days ago, a couple of guys arrived and tried to sneak up on the far side of the trailer when they delivered the big digger, one climbed right up, and we had a hell of a job getting him down. I saw him on the camera from that side, so we got him.'

This guy needs some training, thought Leo, I should have been informed of that, I wonder if he wrote it up in the incident register, I must have a chat to the site foreman.

Then his eyes fastened on one of the many images on the big screen in front of the guard, leaned over the man's shoulder and pointed. 'Pull that one up full size for me, will you?'

They both watched the rain-blurred image of a lone figure walking towards the camera. 'Where is that?'

The guard peered at the screen. 'It's one of the two extra cameras they put up a couple of weeks ago. I haven't got used to them yet. I think that one's a way down along the fence on the south side, where there's a clump of oaks – you know, that place your guys thought someone might try to get over the fence and onto the site, so they put a light up too just for the purpose.'

As they watched, the figure passed the camera and disappeared out of the frame, and Leo frowned. 'Get the next ones up for me, please.'

The guard tapped a couple of keys, and they watched images from two more cameras until the camera aimed alongside the fence outside the main gate showed a hunched form walking slowly towards the gate, limping, head down and hands in pockets. Leo had just said, 'Who the hell is out walking in this weather – and why from that direction?' when the figure turned away from the camera and set off down the road into the darkness beyond the pool of light at the gate. Heavy rain was falling, and the walker was soon out of sight.

Ten minutes later Leo keyed his exit code into the security panel on the portable office he got trucked in a few weeks ago, ran to his car and got in fast before he was drenched. The gate opened for him before he came to a stop at the kiosk, he saluted the guard as he drove away. He was nearly at the crossroads when he spotted someone walking on his side of the road, so he drove slowly past and stopped a short distance ahead. His finger was on the window button and when the walker was level with the front passenger door, he rolled the window down and called out, 'Get in and I'll give you a ride.'

'No, thanks.' The wind was stronger now, and the rain blew sideways. It's a girl, he thought, and she doesn't want to get into a car with a lone male, but this isn't good, she must be frozen, and wet through.

He drove slowly alongside her and called out, 'Don't be stupid, it's long way to town and it's freezing. Get in!'

He had recognised the red wool beanie and the black jacket; it was Sandy, the thorn in his flesh for so long, the girl who was knocked down in the school hall, the girl who exerted such a disturbing pull on his attention. And then she stumbled, lost her balance, and the next moment she was on her knees with both hands on the ground in front of her, and he saw that she had no gloves. He leapt out of the car, caught up to her in three long strides and lifted her with a firm grip on her upper arms.

'For Christ's sake, don't be so bloody stubborn! This is ridiculous, you'll catch your death of cold. I'm trying to help you. Come along!'

He marched her back to the car, opened the door and pushed her into the passenger seat, her weight was no match for his. Running around to the driver's door he thought how ridiculous this instinct to run was when he was already drenched to the skin.

Leaning back in her seat Jamie sat passive and silent, her mind a blank, and Leo leaned across, pulled her seatbelt over and locked it in place. He touched her wet hands. 'You're freezing!' he said and briefly held her hands in a warm clasp, before he let go and pulled out on the road. Jamie felt defeated and couldn't be bothered saying anything. Could anything get else go wrong now? Her life had fallen apart, the protest was over, it had all been in vain, and she was tired and cold.

'Why are you walking in this weather – and alone at that? Did somebody leave without you?'

He reached over and touched her cold hands again and then his hand moved to adjust the heater, aimed it directly at her. She didn't really want to talk to him, but maybe it would do him good to hear how it was on the other side of life. 'My bike got stolen.'

She sensed his head turning towards her. 'Today? At the site?'

'Yes.'

'I'm sorry. I'll get my people to check the CCTV footage. Where did you put it?'

Oh, for God's sake, she thought, don't pretend you care.

'Where did you leave it?' He wasn't going to give in to this stubborn resistance. They were both human beings and taking their battle, that he didn't see as personal, to these lengths was pointless. 'Just tell me.'

'Up against a tree, on the far side of the ditch, but it doesn't matter.'

'Why were you walking along the fence in the dark?'

She hesitated but this might be her only chance to tell him what she thought. 'I wondered if someone might have hidden it to … annoy me, so I walked along the fence to see if they'd hidden it among the trees.'

Security, he thought, she thinks they hid it during the protest. And she must have walked a hell of a long way, that protest broke up ages ago. And why is she limping?

'If that's the case they're for it! I'll check the security footage tomorrow. It's not the sort of behaviour I tolerate.'

He knew he'd be able to see who took it, and when he did, he'd follow up and do something about it.

'I thought you had a car. Why did you ride a bike in this weather?'

'My car got stolen.' She paused for a moment. How did he know she had a car? 'When the police found it, it was burnt out, and …'

'And?'

'Oh, nothing. It's not important.'

They were on the outskirts of town now, in a small pocket of light industry, and suddenly she looked up and recognised where they were. 'Oh, no - please stop, drop me here!'

'Here? I'll take you home.'

'This is where I live.'

Reluctantly he pulled over and looked around. Beside and ahead of them were only dark buildings and workshops, on the other side was the fenced yard of a business selling tractors, shut for the night with spotlights illuminating the vehicles on display. The rain fell in slanting strips of silver under the strong lights.

'You can't live here – let me drive you home.'

'You couldn't live here,' she said cuttingly, goaded into anger, 'but I have to. Thanks for the ride.'

She got out and limped slowly back along the street toward a lane that ran between the buildings, unaware that Leo watched her in the side mirror and only drove off when she has disappeared from sight into the lane. He was still thinking of how cold her hands were.

Chapter 15

Early the next morning Leo entered the guards' hut and tapped the shoulder of the man at the desk. 'Move over for a moment, please. I want to check something from last night.'

While the guard dealt with two trucks presenting paperwork, Leo selected the camera that showed the road outside the main gate. He started playing the footage back from half past four, some time before he was first told that protesters were gathering outside and saw her straight away. It was still only drizzling, and she stood on the side of the road with a group of half a dozen people gathered around her, wearing the black jacket and the high beanie, which was unmistakable. He rewound further, watched the group melt back to only two, Sandy and a man talking beside a car. A bike was leaning against a tree on the other side of the ditch. That must be hers, he said under his breath, so now all I need to do is fast forward and keep an eye on it.

'Still looking?' asked the guard, who wanted his chair back.

'I won't be long.'

While he watched the video run fast through the next half hour of recording, he made a mental note to get the tech company to come back and set things up, so he could access the CCTV footage directly from his desk and his phone.

The group outside the gates grew, the protesters formed lines across the road, then two trucks arrived at the inside of the gates and come to a stop. The first guard tried in vain to reason with the group outside, the second guard appeared and then he himself came into the picture, gestured to the guards to move back, and the talking started. From this point it wasn't long before the situation was under control and the group dispersed. He kept his eyes on the bike, and there he was - a man standing on the edge in the last row, turned and walked back along the side of the road, jumped across the ditch and took the bike, while Leo talked to the young man who had stepped forward to argue.

With a sense of outrage Leo watched the leisurely way the man wheeled the bike down to the little culvert and onto the road, where he swiftly loaded it on the back of a pick-up truck, got in and drove off. Amazingly calm and unhurried, thought Leo, it was all planned, he parked facing away, he knew what he was doing and where to stand to be able to move away from the group without attracting notice. Not a single person turned their head and watched him, all their attention was focused on the negotiations going on up front.

'Do you know how to save a clip from this?' The guard turned around, looked at the screen and shook his head. 'Not a clue,' he said casually and turned back to his window to check a new arrival against his list. Leo found the zoom function and made a note of the pickup truck's number plate and the time stamp.

From childhood Leo had heard his parents raving against authorities and police, social services, and neighbours, indiscriminately berating everyone who had more than they had, whether it was more money, more power or more luck. They were inverted snobs of the worst kind and in his mind, he could hear his dad saying, 'fucking bastards' with vicious emphasis. Now he was going to use his connections and influence and pull a few strings. If his father were alive, he would class Leo with all the others he envied and despised, but what was the point of having influence, if you didn't use it in a good cause?

He knew that in the so-called rural region in the south the small towns no longer had manned police stations, so he called Plymouth and asked to talk to 'someone with decision-making authority and the ability to help prevent a crime', the phrasing deliberately vague. Without protest the woman he talked to put the call through to an inspector.

'I'm aware that my request is out of order,' he said apologetically when he had introduced himself. 'I looked it up and I know I'm supposed to fill in an online form, but this is personal. Yesterday someone stole my visitor's bike that she had left outside the gates at the Vista Resort construction site when she came to see me. I'm trying to find out who took it, so I can get it back for her and I've got the thief's registration plate, it's on our CCTV. I don't expect you to waste your time and manpower on it, and I'm not going to do anything about it apart from retrieve the bike. I think I know why he took it.'

This last was a lie, but he was trying to avoid the police interfering in what he regarded as his business; he wanted to give the impression that he was personally offended that a friend of his had lost her bike on his property.

A couple of minutes later he knew the truck belonged to Trevor Marsh, and soon after he found him on Facebook. Trevor had no privacy settings in place, which allowed Leo to see the pictures he had posted of himself in many situations including one where he stood proudly beside another white pickup truck, this one with the Southwell logo on the door. The photo was captioned 'Made foreman today! Off to celebrate.'

Leo sat unmoving for a few minutes, tried to recall every detail of his conversation with Bill Bridgeman a few weeks ago, the night he had dinner with him and his wife. He played back the last part of that evening in his head, tried to tease out what he had then thought Bill was saying, and how today's discovery had changed that perception.

It had been a tedious evening with constant sniping between Bill and Wendy. Leo was the only guest, Bill drank too much and got boastful and loud, and Wendy, whom Leo had not met previously, pursed her lips and made snide comments about how fat he was getting and how he much he was drinking. After turning down the offer of a cognac after dinner, just when Leo thought he could safely say goodnight and go home, Bill had said, 'You've got to know who your friends are, Leo!' and tapped the side of his nose. 'There's nothing as important as friends, you know. Sometimes a friend can do you a favour, no harm done, just because they can.'

He winked at Leo and Wendy glared at him. 'For God's sake Bill – what are you talking about? When you drink you get to be like some mystic oracle and nobody can make sense of what you say.'

'Now, now – no need to be rude, dear. I'm just saying Leo and I both know what matters. Nothing's as important as favours between friends.'

Now Leo stared unseeing out of his window where a bulldozer trundled slowly past, making his office shake. What had he thought at the time? Nothing much, he decided, just that Bill was trying to impress him or possibly influence him, well aware that very soon the tender period for the stage one landscaping contract for the resort would open. And Bill was keen to get the contact, which would be the biggest job Southwell's had ever been involved in. It would keep their entire workforce flat out for a year or two, working on one stage after another. But now Leo thought of Sandy telling him that her car had been stolen and found torched, and her bike brazenly taken by a Southwell employee. Coincidence or an indication of a personal vendetta on his behalf?

He called the surveillance company that had installed the cameras and asked them to send him the video clip of the five minutes around the theft of the bike. 'And can you also send someone over to install whatever software I need, so I can see both live and archived footage on my laptop and my phone?'

At ten past four he walked into Southwell's administration building and asked for Trevor Marsh. 'He's out at a work site,' said the woman behind the desk. 'Can someone else help you?'

'No, thanks. I'll catch up with him another time.'

'Would you like him to call you?' There was avid curiosity in her eyes, and he was well aware that everyone around here knew him by sight, so she would be wondering why he was standing in Southwell's office for the first time but not asking for Bill Bridgeman.

'Is he coming back here at the end of the day?'

'No, the site's way out on the other side of town, near Loddiswell – he'll go straight home, he lives out that way.'

Leo went back to his car and used his phone to check

Southwell's website for photos of past and current projects. When Bill first made overtures of friendship, Leo had looked up the firm online and he remembered the listing of projects. Half an hour later he parked at a construction site near Loddiswell and walked down a narrow, sloping access road to a gate with a sign saying, 'Work vehicles only, no unauthorized access.'

The gate was open, and there was nobody in sight, so he returned to the car and watched the gate in his side mirror. Fifteen minutes later from around the corner of a portacabin, a pickup truck approached; white with the distinctive bright blue S in a circle on the door, the Southwell logo. Leo got out and raised his hand in the universal 'stop' signal and the driver pulled up beside him.

'Trevor Marsh?' he said, though he knew the answer. 'Can I have a word?'

'Of course, Mr Masters – I'll just pull over so the stragglers can get past. Still a couple of guys putting stuff away.'

Marsh climbed out of his truck, unsure of what to expect and perhaps a bit apprehensive, and Leo looked him straight in the eye and said, 'Where is the bike?'

Marsh's eyes slid away to look over Leo's shoulder. 'Ah, I'm not sure what you mean.'

'You know damn well what I mean. We've got you on security video stealing a bike last night at our site gates. Where is it?' Now his voice carried a note of menace and Marsh flinched.

'Ok, ok - but I was told to take it. I just did was I was told.'

Leo never took his eyes off Trevor's face. 'Who asked you to take it?'

Marsh's expression was one of fear and indecision; he opened his mouth and closed it again.

'Well? Who told you to take the bike?'

'I can' tell you … it's confidential, I'll get into trouble.'

Leo took two steps closer, backed Marsh up against the cab of his truck and used his anger to intimidate him. 'Not as much trouble as you could be in right now! Was it Bridgeman?'

He read the answer on Marsh's face before he reluctantly said, 'Yeah, he said it was a favour for you.'

'Like hell it was! Is he paying you?'

And again, the answer was written on Marsh's face. 'Right.' Leo's voice was hard. 'Now we know where we stand. I can report you for theft and use the CCTV video as evidence. Or we can make a deal – it's up to you.'

He watched in silence while Marsh processed the pros and cons of the ultimatum, then after a long pause he cleared his throat. 'Let's make a deal.'

'Listen carefully, now – this is what's going to happen. You will mention absolutely nothing about this to anyone, not to anyone at all, not to your wife or your best mate. Tomorrow morning, before you head back out here, you will drop a sealed envelope with the money Bridgeman paid you at the admin office – with Bridgeman's name on it. I presume he paid you in cash? OK - if he asks why, you'll say it didn't feel right and you regret accepting it. Nothing more – not one single word.'

Marsh nodded, uneasy and uncertain. 'OK. Are you going to tell him you know?'

'What I do is my business, and you don't need to know. But I can practically guarantee that Bridgeman won't dare question you or ever mention it again. And I won't report you for theft if you give me the bike.'

'He'll sack me - like he sacked that girl a while ago.'

'I don't think he will, but if he does, I'll give you a job, you know where to find me. Now get back in your truck and I'll follow you to wherever you dropped that bike.'

Marsh simply nodded. This happened very fast, and he hadn't had time to process the implications. His expression reflected his chaotic emotions: his fear of both the power and the physical presence of Leo, his apprehension about Bridgeman's reaction, his relief at Leo's promise of a job.

The bike was still where Marsh left it behind two shipping containers at the back of an empty building, in the same area where Leo had dropped Sandy the night before. Leo opened the back of his SUV and nodded at Marsh, who silently loaded the bike into it.

'How did you know she was going to ride her bike, or even where she was going to be?'

'Mr Bridgeman knew about the plan for the group to go to the site. He just said for me to go and see if I could do some mischief.' He thought for a moment and added, 'He did mention the girl – he doesn't like her, so I thought I'd nick the bike, I've seen her on it.'

'OK. You know where to find me if he sacks you. Now go!' was all he said, before he got into his car and waited for Marsh to drive out of the yard; he turned left, and Leo turned right.

Leo parked at the entrance to the lane close to where he stopped the previous evening, lifted the bike out and walked it along the road. He left it halfway down the little alleyway and continued along it, looking closely at the buildings and the windows. There was no sign of the kind of windows a flat would have, mostly blank walls of brick and concrete, or windows up high. The lane came out on a street with the same kind of small industries, and Leo stood indecisive and wondered if she just used the lane to get to the road on this side, and maybe she didn't live anywhere near the lane itself. He turned to go back the way he had come. Dusk was falling now, and he couldn't think of what to do next. And then he spotted the rusty iron stairs on the second to last building on the left side of the lane and looked up. And there, at the top of the third short zig zag flight, was a door and beside it two windows, one much smaller than the other. The building was only one and a half storey high, and he guessed that the space at the top of the stairs was a mezzanine floor. just enough room under the sloping roof for a little flat.

Maybe this is it, he thought and looked at the bike he had left leaning against a wall further down the lane. Wouldn't it be the ultimate frustration if someone nicked it now? He jogged down and wheeled the bike right up to the stairs and tucked it in against the wall where it wouldn't be so noticeable.

At the door on the top landing, he raised his hand to knock and hesitated. Leaning sideways over the rail, as far to the right as possible and looking into the window at an angle, he could see a wedge of the interior. A small light was on somewhere in the hidden part of the room; just inside the window a black jacket hung over the back of a chair with a red knitted hat resting on one shoulder.

He retreated, made sure the bike was nearly invisible between the stairs and the wall and returned to his car. Half an hour later he was back with a bike lock from the supermarket. He walked quietly down the lane, set the combination lock to the last four digits of his cellphone number and locked the bike to the fire stairs. On the outside of the white bag the lock came in, he wrote in large capitals: *Your bike is at the bottom of the stairs. The lock code is 0166.* He climbed up and tied the plastic bag to the railing where she couldn't miss it the next time she came out of her the door.

Chapter 16

First thing the following morning Leo entered Southwell Landscaping's office, turned down the receptionist's offer of assistance and walked straight past her. Without knocking he pushed open the door and entered Bridgeman's office and Bill exclaimed, "Leo! How nice to see you, my friend, how are you?'

'Morning, Bill. Apologies for barging in, but this has got to be said face to face. Listen carefully - if you want to have the slightest chance of getting the contract for the resort, you will never do another so-called bloody favour for me!'

Bridgeman pushed his chair back and got up, his face expressed a mixture of concern and a hint of fear. 'Leo! I can't imagine what ...' and Leo stepped around the corner of the desk, right up close so Bill had to tilt his head back to look up into his face.

'I know far more than you think, Bill, and I am very angry! If I hear of anything being done again on my behalf, by you or anyone else who's in any way connected to you, there will be serious trouble.'

The cold fury in Leo's eyes made Bill flinch and he took a fast step back and opened his mouth to speak, but Leo silenced him with a look, turned and walked out of the door he left open when he arrived.

As he drove away, he tried to imagine the scene in Bill's office at that moment. Was Bill swearing and throwing things, had the receptionist already given him Marsh's envelope and had she told him Leo had asked for Marsh yesterday? Was Bill connecting the dots, calling Marsh? I don't give a shit, said Leo out loud. He's a nasty piece of work and I'll not waste any time on him.

Leo realised that arriving unannounced was probably not the best way of getting to see inspector Grindle, but as he had to be in Plymouth on business anyway, he might as well try before going back to Kingsbridge. But luck was on his side and he only waited twenty minutes before Grindle is free to see him.

'Mr Masters, what can I do for you?' Grindle shook his hand and gestured at the door he had just come out of. 'Come in and sit down.'

My Dad would be sneering, thought Leo, as he followed Grindle through the door beside the reception desk, but this is what makes the world go around: contacts and networks, favours to be called in. You'd have to be mad not to use them if they're available.

Grindle showed Leo into a small room with a glass

wall to a large open work area with computers on desks cluttered with files and coffee mugs. A large silver and red balloon on a stick with 40 in large red print was attached to the side of one desk.

'I have business in Plymouth today, and I thought I'd ask another favour. Does your station check all the minor crimes that are reported from the region? Like car thefts in Kingsbridge, for example.'

'All incidents are entered into the system and get looked at by us and we review everything that happens in the greater area. But anything in the system can be seen from any station in the country. Are you thinking of something specific?'

'You were very helpful when my visitor's bike was stolen at the Vista Resort site and thanks to you, we got the bike back. The guy has apologized, no harm done. He was set up by someone else, just a pawn. Now, just before that happened, my friend's car was stolen and torched. It was taken from Kingsbridge, where she lives. And I've begun to wonder if she's being harassed as a message to me. You've probably heard of the unpleasant meeting in the Wellby school hall, when a young woman was injured.'

Leo rehearsed this partially fictitious version of the story on the way to Plymouth, mostly factual but with hints that Grindle can interpret as he liked.

'Ah!' said Grindle. 'Now I see the connection. Let me look it up and see if there's anything new on that car theft. I do remember it because they set fire to it, which was a bit of a surprise, it's usually just someone wanting to go joy riding and doing doughnuts on the open road, and then we find the car more or less undamaged a couple of days later.'

Leo got up and read the diplomas and commendations on the walls, mentally crossing his fingers that this wouldn't go wrong, while Grindle checked things on his computer.

'I see you were awarded the Queen's Police Medal – that must have been for something special.'

Grindle's eyes were on his computer screen and he said absently, 'God knows why I got it, just a bit of nasty drama. Ah yes, here we are - the car was reported stolen by Alexandra Jamieson. I presume that's who we're talking about. Yes? We have no further information, I'm sorry to say. Do you think it might have been the same man who took the bike?'

So that's her full name, Alexandra Jamieson, thought Leo, known as Sandy. Thank God, he didn't ask me for her full name, I had a contingency plan, but it was far from perfect.

'No, I'm pretty sure it wasn't him - he was more of a victim than a criminal, got pushed into taking the bike by somebody else. I think I can guarantee he'll never do anything like it again.'

'Hmm,' said Grindle and looked Leo in the eye, and now he was back in serious police mode. 'I hope that doesn't mean that any violence took place when you got the bike back.'

Leo returned the look with a straight face. 'I didn't

touch him. I might have inadvertently scared him, but I never issued any threats.'

Grindle tried to hide a smile and failed, and Leo got to his feet. 'Thanks for your help! I know Sandy would have been told if you'd found something out, but seeing I was in the neighbourhood I thought I'd call in and introduce myself and say thanks for helping with that number plate. And to let you know that I got the bike back. If there's anything I can do in return, please let me know.'

He sat in the car for a long time thinking about Bridgeman and the bike theft and wondering if the car theft was set up by him too, maybe using someone else. Would he dare go that far? It was a big step from hiding a bike to stealing and setting fire to a car. Leo had heard that there was a bit of drug trade in Kingsbridge, it had been mentioned at a Vista progress meeting not long ago. Presumably some drug users would do nearly anything for money, and Bill probably knew more or less everyone in the wider area. There was nothing Leo could do about it, but he could have another chat to Marsh to find out what he might have heard. And it's nice to know her full name, he thought, that might well be useful sometime in the future.

Chapter 17

Jamie opened the glass washer and lifted out the basket in a cloud of moist heat, put it on the tiled bench top and picked up a glass towel. It was unusually quiet, and she thought idly it was probably inevitable in the autumn with fewer holiday makers.

Only four tables were occupied, and nobody stood at the bar, but it was still early. She picked up a glass that was nearly too hot to handle and checked it against the light, wiped a drop off the rim and put it in its rack. When the music stopped, she walked toward the corner to restart it and a stray phrase from the table close to that end of the bar caught her attention. She decided to leave the music off for a moment, took a couple of steps back and picked up another glass and turned so she could hear better.

'No, no, it's not like swapping it for low grade stuff,' said the older of the two men at the table. 'It's not going to make anything collapse, don't worry. But those steel specifications are way too rigid, makes everything overengineered. Some structural steel importers don't bother getting the certification – it costs megabucks and I've got good contacts with the company Vista's buying from. I'm not sure how the importers get around some of the regulations, these guys stock both kinds, with and without the certification stamp, and they sell lots of both.'

Jamie quickly processed what she heard against articles she had read and made a snap decision. She put down the second glass, which she has been polishing endlessly while she listened and pulled her phone out of her apron pocket. Quickly she turned it on to video, put it on the bar top as close as possible to the men and hoped it would record the conversation.

'So how the hell would it work?' asked the other man suspiciously. 'Materials are checked off as correct against the inwards goods list when they're delivered, so where in the process does the switch take place.'

'Don't worry about the logistics. We've got that sorted and it does work, believe me! At most sites nobody checks the stamp on the steel to match it against the delivery manifest, which makes it simple. All we need is you onsite ticking it off as conforming to the listing, which it will do, everything will match, apart from the actual code stamped on the girders. And then when the invoice arrives, some clerical girl checks it against the delivery docket number you initialled, and there you go, all done! And the bill gets paid in full, but the difference gets split three ways between the importer, me and you.'

'So, you've done this before? And it worked? I just don't understand why it doesn't get noticed.'

'Four times now, mate! Totally safe, nobody suspected a thing. On this monster project you could earn yourself forty thousand at least, but it's up to you.'

'OK, it's too good to pass up, but if it goes wrong at my end, I'm not going down alone. I'll tell them who you are, if it turns to shit!'

This was even more serious even than it seemed at the start, so Jamie picked up her phone and angled it as if she was taking a selfie, with the camera filming through the lens on the back. As she struck a pretend selfie pose, she checked on the screen that she was capturing the men, waited until they were both clearly visible and put the phone back on the bar, where it continued recording. Two couples came in, so she moved the phone and attended to them, and by the time they were seated at a table, the two men had left.

She spent the rest of the evening trying to make up her mind about what to do. That the conversation had serious implications for the Vista project was obvious, and she tried to work through how it might play out. If the substandard steel wasn't discovered until after it had been installed, perhaps when some inspection took place, it could result in part of a structure having to be demolished and rebuilt. Expensive, she thought, and it would delay the completion of the resort, which might have greater consequences that just the monetary cost. It might affect the reputation of LM Construction, put other projects in jeopardy and cast doubt on Leo Master's reputation. If the switch was discovered before the steel had become part of a building, the consequences would presumably be far less damaging. She couldn't find it in herself to do nothing, to let it happen. Her objections to the Vista Resort could not be allowed to influence her decision of right and wrong. Should she tell Leo Masters first or the council who issued the building permit, or the police? That she has a moral obligation to tell someone was a given, and though she really didn't want to have anything more to do with Leo Masters, he deserved to know. As soon as an investigation started, the media would pick up on it and turn it into a scandal, and because he was a high-profile person, they would make it personal. She wouldn't discuss this with anyone in the protest group. Brent would dive on it like a starving seagull, but that wouldn't be fair to anyone. She would find out which authority issued the building permit and a bit more about the steel grades over the weekend, but she would tell Leo Masters first.

Chapter 18

When Jamie greeted a party of six at the restaurant on the Saturday evening, it seemed that fate had given her a perfect opportunity. Two married couples that she recognised from previous occasions, a stunning looking young woman and Leo Masters. She showed them to their table, very aware of Leo's attention on her and tried to not look directly at him when she handed them menus and wine lists. She returned to the desk, grateful that he was sitting side-on to her and watched out of the corner of her eye as he studied the menu with his head turned towards the girl beside him and then beckoned to the wine waiter. What a perfect couple they made those two. Both dark and striking looking and just what she would have expected from him, a woman at least fifteen years younger and gorgeous, probably no more than twenty or twenty-two. And not from Kingsbridge, thought Jamie, or I would surely have noticed her before. I might get a chance to intercept him if he gets up from the table before the others or perhaps as they leave. I'd rather warn him in person than call his office and try to tell him about it on the phone. If I can corner him discretely and make him listen to the recording, he must believe me.

The irony of her desire to give him a chance to be the first to reveal the fraud conspiracy wasn't lost on her. As a staunch opponent of the Vista development, she might be expected to try to embarrass him as much as possible, instead she was trying to shield him. She told herself it wasn't because she fancied him or because he had been to kind to her in the rain, it's just doing what is right and fair.

Despite how late in the season it was, Saturday evening was busy and things were complicated by a number of casual diners arriving; two couples happy to wait in the bar for a table to become free, and some who thought she should be able to conjure up a table out of thin air. Time passed quickly and suddenly Jamie noticed that the party Leo Masters was with were already having dessert. Damn, she thought, and I never even saw if he got up, but he probably didn't – it's usually only women, or men who get drunk, who go the restroom. But a few minutes later he did get up with his phone in his hand and she watched him head for the door. He walked right past her desk, talking in a low voice and disappeared around the corner towards the bar, and Jamie made a snap decision. Quickly she gestured to the wine waiter, who was experienced and knew the routines. 'Can you please watch the desk for a moment? I'll be back in five.'

She used the kitchen corridor and made a right angle turn to emerge in the foyer, just by the entrance to the bar, and waited until Leo Masters ended the call.

'Mr Masters, excuse me.' Her voice was pitched slightly too high. How odd, she had time to think, I didn't realise I'm a bit nervous, but so long as he doesn't realise that I'm Sandy the protester, I don't care what I sound like.

'Yes?' He waited until she was right next to him, and suddenly she didn't know how to start, acutely uncomfortable about confronting him in a place like this. And standing close to him brought it home that he wasn't just a figure head to do battle with over an issue, but a very attractive male. So instead of trying to explain or even introduce herself, she just got her phone out and said, 'Please wait a moment – there is something you need to listen to.'

He waited, expressionless and silent, while she found the video. 'Here, start it playing and listen to the first part. I couldn't film them at first, but I did get their faces later in the recording. I've set the sound level quite low.'

She held out the phone and as he took it from her their fingers touched and made her jump. It was the same sensation as when he touched her frozen hands in the car, she wanted the touch to never end. The look he gave her told her nothing, it must be a one-sided sensation on her part; now she felt more unnerved than ever.

'OK,' he said and held the phone close to his head,

but as he listened his expression slowly changed. He pause the recording and handed her the phone. 'Can you please go forward to the place where you filmed them?'

She fast forwarded and had a pretty good idea of where it was because she has looked at those faces several times since Thursday. 'Here, I've paused it where you can see them best. It's all one recording, but most of it's only audio. I did an Internet search for their faces, but I didn't find them.'

He took the phone again and looked down at the freeze-frame image for a moment, his lips tightened and a deep crease appeared between his eyebrows. 'I've seen both these men somewhere, obviously one of them works for us, though I don't know which one. I wonder where I've seen the other guy.'

'The one who works for you is the younger one,' said Jamie. 'I was looking their way as I listened. He was the one being recruited.'

They looked at each other for a moment; he was appalled, and she was relieved that he had listened. Suddenly she felt a need to explain it in more detail, though she knew it didn't matter, it was just a feeling she had that she wanted him to understand what had motivated her to record the conversation.

'At the start, when I first realised that they were talking about fraud, but before I started recording them, they mentioned a certificate of some kind relating to the steel. The older man said something like "it doesn't mean it's not good steel, nothing will collapse" so I presumed that it referred to the quality certification and possibly fake grade stamps on the steel.'

She felt, as much as saw, how his focus on her intensified and inside she was amused. He was surprised she knew that kind of thing, even though it had been in the news several times in the last couple of years. Maybe he realised she must have done some online research about steel, and he was surprised at that.

Leo Masters was still holding her phone. 'May I put my number in your contacts list? And then you can send me a text, so I have yours. This is very serious, thank you for alerting me. I presume you'll let me have the recording?'

'Of course. I'll send it, but email might be better than attaching it to a text.'

'OK, I'll reply to your text and give you my personal email address. And thank you again! What's your name?'

'Jamie. And by the way, I haven't reported this - I'm leaving that to you.'

She went back the way she came, via the corridor behind the foyer and stopped for a moment to catch her breath and make sure she was calm. That man is so dangerous, she thought, before she returned to her desk, so attractive and so powerful, and with such a compelling presence. I've never met anyone like him before.

Later that night she sat on her bed and checked the contacts list in her phone, so she could text him and saw 'Masters', which was all he has entered along with his number. Her mind seemed to freeze for a moment and she stared at the screen. His number ended with the same four figures that unlocked her bike lock, the code the person who returned her bike set up – 0166. How was this possible? It wasn't even worth considering that it might be a random coincidence. The bike turning up like that, with a lock and the bag tied to the railing with the number written on it; the most baffling thing that ever happened to her. She had spent a lot of time puzzling over it, but this was a total surprise.

She sat on her bed and re-lived the timeline of what happened: she told him in the car that the bike got stolen, he went out and located the bike, worked out where she lived, bought the lock and left the message on the bag tied to the rail. Why? Did he know all along where the bike was? Did it mean that he knew she was the same person as Sandy, the protester? And if he did know, and if she met him again, say if he wanted to talk to her, she would be at a disadvantage.

Chapter 19

Jamie was walking to the supermarket to get her dinner, which was her new way of living. Having no fridge meant either dry-packaged dinner, canned food or buying fresh and eating it that day. Today was a fresh food day, the best kind, and she was thinking of what she wanted to eat. She had bought a glass microwavable dish, so she could make small casserole style dinners. It made her feel that she was a normal person with a marginally normal life, that being practically unemployed and living in her ghastly room didn't define her as a person. It had taken a couple of weeks before she had realised how much her sense of being a failure and having let herself down stemmed from the lack of meaning and function, having nothing to do. She had so much time on her hands now and in her room, there was nothing to do apart from read. She felt as if the real world had discarded her, and the lives of others were playing out elsewhere, in a place she couldn't reach.

It had been a cool and windy day, well into autumn now, but the sun had shone and every day the sky was blue was a better day. Lately she had come to understand that now the weather influenced her mood to a far greater degree than before, how a blue-sky day made her feel more positive.

It would be great to live somewhere with an Internet connection, so she didn't have to read the news on her phone, which is her only way of catching up with things now. It's too cramped, she thought and turned the collar on her jacket up, and the lines of text are so short on the phone, it's a really irritating way of reading things, you lose the flow of the text. News headlines and short items, yes, but not continuous text. She had never understood how Gemma could read entire novels on her phone, it didn't bother her at all, though admittedly Gemma's phone had a much bigger screen.

Just then the phone in her pocket made the double beep alert for a text. From Leo Masters, which was a surprise. She hadn't expected to hear anything more from him after he sent his reply thanking her for the email with the recording.

'Jamie, can we please meet, either more or less now, or later this evening or tomorrow? I want to fill you in on developments and buy you a drink as a token thank you. Leo'

Well, I can keep it brief, Jamie told herself, there's no need to make it a social event, because I think the best thing for my peace of mind is to spend as little time as possible near Leo. That touch of his fingers nearly set me on fire. She stopped at the corner and texted a reply. *'I'm close to the King's Arms right now, will wait for you there.'*

Leo arrived at the pub ten minutes after Jamie, who was looking at her phone and didn't see him come in.

'Hi, Jamie,' he said, 'What will you have to drink?'

She looked up, thought how expressionless his face often was, and wondered if it was deliberate or just the way his face was made. She smiled. 'A glass of chardonnay please.'

He returned with two glasses of wine and now he smiled too. 'I've ordered tapas - I didn't have time to eat lunch today and I'm starving.'

God, the transformation, his whole face changed when he smiled and his eyes crinkled in a way that made her want to smile back. But instead of smiling back, she waited for him to speak, well aware of how he seemed to draw her towards him and not about to allow herself to become fixated on him, but he just took a drink of his wine and said nothing.

This would be slightly unsettling, Jamie felt, if it wasn't for the fact that he was in her debt and he had invited her, so it was up to him to say something. If he thought she was going to start chatting about nothing, this would go nowhere. But she had to admit, though only to herself, that she was disturbed by her own reactions to him. It was like a physical force, possibly just lust, but very powerful.

'That recording of yours,' he said after a moment.

'It's a bombshell, which of course you know, but I'd be very interested to know how this came about. Those guys obviously had a bit of an exchange about the steel already, before the recording starts, which alerted you, you told me about that at The Anchorage, but you caught the crucial part. Where were you – at the next table?'

'Oh no, I was working, I was doing the evening shift in the bar. I don't like the bar work, but I need more work than the single shift they've let me keep in the restaurant. But to get back to your first question.'

She drank some of her wine and waited while the barman delivered a large platter of tapas and thought that solved the problem of her dinner. 'I was emptying the glass washer and the music came to an end, and in the little silence – there were hardly any customers there at that stage – I heard a couple of sentences that seemed … it sounded strange, suspicious. People speak louder than they realise when they're in a place with background music and if the music stops, they don't change their voice, or not instantly.'

'Was that the bit you mentioned, about the certificate?'

Perversely she decided it would do her morale a lot of good to maybe surprise him again and make him realise she wasn't the person he had thought. 'They'd already attracted my attention before that, but the talk about grade certificates decided me, because it's been written about quite a lot in the last few years. I remembered reading about the steel girders holding up huge structures like stadium or hangar roofs and how they can buckle and collapse in an intense fire if they're not the right grade steel. I knew I had to get some kind of proof of what they were planning.'

His focus on her now was so intense it felt like sunburn, but all he said was, 'And?'

'So, I turned the phone camera on to video, to record and put it on the bar which is why you only see darkness for a while. I put it lens down and screen up because the microphone is on the front. I just had to hope it would pick up the conversation without me holding it up. And I didn't restart the music, of course, and then after a little while I worked out how to get their faces too, so I did that.'

'Yes?'

He's a demon for short questions, thought Jamie and drank some more of her wine, and watched him over the rim of the glass. But it's just his nature, I think, he doesn't sound impatient.

'I pretended I was taking a selfie, which by the way I never do, but I've seen the poses people strike, so I did the same. Held the phone up with my arm out straight, but of course the camera was filming through the lens on the back, and I could see on the screen when I had the angle right.'

'Very quick thinking,' said Leo and smiled again. 'Very clever – and I can't tell you how grateful I am. My managers and I sat down and looked at it on a bigger screen and we've identified the man who was being recruited, as you put it. I thought I recognised his face, but my HR manager could put a name to him nearly immediately, she did the initial screening when the jobs were advertised. He only started a few weeks ago.'

'And?' said Jamie with a straight face, and Leo grinned appreciatively. 'I'm calling him in for a meeting tomorrow. I'll sack him, of course. I've already reported the whole thing to the police and to the steel importer. They'll have to sort out their own mess and work out who the middleman is. And I've informed the UK Steel Standards organization too.'

'Good – and the man you're meeting with tomorrow, the one who works for you, is he local?'

'No, he's not, but I think you know his father-in-law.'

'What? Who would that be?'

'He's the senior partner in the law firm where you work.'

It took a few seconds for Jamie to work out the connection and it made her laugh, here was the final act in the comedy of errors.

'Oh, of course, you think I work there! I don't, I was there as a client and the receptionist had to dash off in a hurry. And then the phone rang, and nobody seemed to be answering it from some other room, so I picked it up and took a message – and then you turned up.'

She stopped and looked down at the platter of tapas between them, suddenly she remembered the look of impatience on his face when she failed to put a call through. Her smile faded, she could still feel the embarrassment, even though they both knew now that it wasn't a failing on her part. But she said it anyway. 'And you thought I was incompetent.'

'I'm sorry I was so impatient, I really am,' he said, surprising her. 'I'm not normally an impatient person, but it was a very fraught day and I urgently needed to see Jordan. I regretted being so brusque nearly immediately, and I was going to apologize, but when I came out from Jordan's room you weren't there. And I didn't know you had just stepped in to help.'

She didn't reply; she's looking at someone to the left of his shoulder and then her eyes slid away and down to the table between them.

'What's wrong?'

'Nothing.' She was still only just looking at him. He swung around in his chair and caught the eye of a man, who was looking straight at Jamie with a smug smile.

'Is that guy bothering you?'

She tried to brush it off, she knew that to most people her reasons for being apprehensive about the man would seem flimsy. 'I don't like him, and he knows it, he …'

'Yes? He …?'

'I'm not sure, but he seems to turn up a lot, but it's probably just that I notice him because I don't like the way he looks at me.' And for the first time it occurred to her, that if his behavior was deliberate, he was a stalker.

'Is he stalking you?' asked Leo, as if he had read her mind. 'If he is, I don't mind going over there to have a word with him.'

'Oh, no, please don't!' She was instantly alarmed at the thought of the man being given a reason to resent her. 'Please don't do that! It might make him worse.'

'Come on.' Leo got to his feet and picked up his glass and the platter. 'Let's move further away.'

He led the way to a table in the corner where they were hidden from most of the room, and pulled out a chair, so Jamie could sit with her back to the bar. 'Is that better?'

She thanked him and he continued as if nothing unusual had happened. 'So where do you work, apart from at the restaurant. From what you said it sounds as if you've lost some of your shifts there?'

'My full-time job was at Southwell Landscaping.' She hesitated for a moment before she decided to continue, but maybe he needed to understand that protesting wasn't just a hobby, it had serious consequences for some. 'I was sacked. Mr Bridgeman said I was acting contrary to the interests of the business.'

She studied his face and reflected how strange this conversation was, like something out of Alice in Wonderland. She knew some things, and he knew others, and in some respects, they were fumbling in the dark as they tried to work out what connected the facts that were emerging.

After a moment of silence, he exclaimed, 'My God, you're the girl I picked up in the rain, aren't you? Sandy, the protester, whose bike was stolen - and I never made the connection.' Surprising them both, he reached out and puts his hand on hers. 'Your hands were like ice!'

She smiled. 'And you got my bike back and locked it to the stairs. I noticed the last four digits of your phone number were the same as the lock combination. Did you know where I live?'

'No, but I worked it out. I went up those rickety stairs and I saw your jacket and the red beanie on the chair by the window, so I knew it was your place.'

'Thank you for finding the bike – or *did* one of your guys take it?'

'No, but I checked our CCTV footage the next morning and saw a man put it on a pickup truck while we were all busy talking at the gate, so I got the cops to tell me who owns the truck. He works for Southwell's – well past tense, he used to work for them. Bridgeman paid him to harass the protesters, mentioned you and told this guy that he was doing a favour for me. So, I had a go at the bike thief - and then I went and had a go at Bridgeman too, the bastard.'

She contemplated his face, looked him up and down, and grinned. 'I can imagine you doing that – you probably gave him heart failure. I wish I could have seen it! And will Bridgeman still have a chance to get the contract for the Vista site now?'

'He might, but only if he comes in with a spectacularly good tender. I've told him I want no further so-called favours from him, and if there's any more of that kind, he'll have no chance at all. And you might be interested to know that the man, who stole the bike, was sacked and now he works for me. Yes, I can see what you think, but I don't think he'll ever fall for the temptation to do something bad for money again. And he knows his job

– not to mention that he knows my foreman's keeping an eye on him.'

'If I ask you a question, will you promise to answer with a straight yes or no?' She knew this might be the end of a surprisingly pleasant and possibly temporary acquaintance, but she really wanted to know.

He nodded. 'Of course.'

'Did you organize the countermarch when we did the street march?'

'No.'

'Good.'

'Did you think I had? It's not the kind of thing I would do – vengeful and mean.'

'No, I realise that now, or at least I didn't think you would, and I never thought you were vengeful or mean. Some of the others said it was probably set up by you, but I think it was that group of rednecks who started the brawl in the hall.'

'Tell me why you live above that factory. It doesn't seem safe.'

'I know, but I couldn't afford to stay where I was, and it's hard to find anything good that's really cheap. I call it the ghastly garret, and it *is* dirt cheap.'

She rose and so did he. 'Thanks for the drink and the food!'

She glanced towards the bar and saw that the man who stared at her had gone. Leo noticed her look and said calmly, 'He left about ten minutes ago, I made sure he knew I was keeping an eye on him. But how is the wound in your head? I never realised you were hurt at the time, and then I saw that hideous picture in the paper. I wish I'd known!'

She lifted her hair up and showed him the long red scar close to the hairline, and it felt like an intimate thing to do, which she didn't realise until she had done it. 'It took ages to heal, but I had some of those wound strips, so I put them across it and replaced them every couple of days.'

He dropped her off at the end of the lane and sat watching until she had climbed the stairs and closed the door behind her. On an impulse he drove around the block twice, but he didn't see the man from the bar.

For the first time since she moved here, Jamie pulled the curtains over the window. She wonders what Leo meant when he said, 'I wish I'd known!'

Chapter 20

At quarter past seven the following evening, Grindle called Leo just after he arrived home. 'I'm sorry to be the bearer of bad news,' he said with the sound of traffic behind him. 'I'm at the hospital in Plymouth and Miss Jamieson has just been brought in by ambulance. She's had a bad fall and they're doing X-rays and scans now. Because I know she's a friend of yours I checked, and she seems to have no next of kin. I thought you'd want to know.'

'Is she badly hurt? What happened?

'I don't know how serious it is, she's having scans as we speak, and I never saw her. Serious enough, she was unconscious when she was found. She was lying in an alleyway between some commercial buildings in Kingsbridge, at the bottom of an external flight of stairs apparently. The ambulance crew called us.'

'Thank you, I'll be there as soon as I can. How did you come to hear of it – not what you usually do, is it?

'No, it was pure coincidence. I'm here visiting my brother, who had surgery yesterday and when I was leaving I met an officer I know just outside and he told me he'd been called to an accident scene by the ambulance crew, he had come along after the ambulance to get some details of who she was. The paramedics thought it might have been a robbery, like a bag snatcher, but it appears she fell from the stairs, her bag was still at the top.'

Leo didn't ask for any further details, he just thanked Grindle and thought for a moment before he put the laptop back in his satchel, picked up his rain jacket and left for Plymouth.

'No, I mean *now*,' said Leo a couple of hours later. 'I know you have a care plan in place already, and I'm sorry to butt in at this stage, but unless there's some acute medical reason why she can't be moved, which you've just told me there isn't, she's going to The Oaks private hospital, I've just talked to them. She has no family and she is my fiancé and I'm paying for it.'

The doctor met his eyes, gave him a wry smile and nodded. 'All right —we'll organize the transfer, but you'll have to pay for the ambulance. We'll send the scan results and the X-ray of her arm over to The Oaks, so they have all the information. As I told you earlier, we sedated her to stop her thrashing around, she was very muddled and restless, and we had to keep her quiet for the scan.'

He knew she was irritated by his insistence to move

Jamie tonight, that she thought he was just flexing his muscles and being pushy.

'I'm sorry to be so demanding,' he said and smiled. 'I know it seems mad, and it's not because I don't trust you to do the right thing, but she's very special, and someone's been harassing her. I don't know if this fall had anything to do with that, but I'm not taking any chances. At The Oaks I can make sure nobody gets near her. She'll be in a single room, and I can be right beside her the whole time. If this fall wasn't an accident, I'm not prepared to take any risks.'

They parted on good terms and he sat down again to wait for the promised ambulance.

Leo was sitting in the corner, where he'd been since the previous evening with his laptop on a tray table a nurse brought in for him. From there he could see Jamie's face and he wasn't in the way when the nursing staff come in to check on her. Amazing, he thought sleepily, how many emails you can respond to and how many problems you can sort out, when you're not working from home or from your office. No distractions, no interruptions and nothing to tempt you away from the task in front of you. And access to an endless supply of espresso coffee and biscuits, not what I'd have got at the NHS hospital.

Jamie seemed to be sleeping quietly on her back with one arm in a plaster cast from the wrist nearly to the elbow, but in her nightmare, she was fighting for her life. She pushed the man away, but he grabbed her arm. She managed to hang on to the railing with her other hand, then she fell on the hard metal steps, she desperately tightened her fingers, tried to retain her grip. He took hold one of her ankles, and she tried to kick him with her free leg, but her foot was caught in something, and she couldn't get it lose. He pulled harder, tried to drag her down the stairs towards him … and then she was falling and twisting in the air, she screamed and her arms flailed, but there was nothing to hold on to.

Leo's head snapped up and he was on his knees beside her only seconds after she hit the floor. The sheet was tangled around her legs and caught under her, and her eyes were open, but she didn't see him. She was still in a dream of terror and panic, her breathing rapid and panting, her head twisting from side to side.

'Shush,' he said quietly, 'don't be frightened, Jamie, it's all right now, I'm here.'

He held her head between his hands and stroked his thumbs over her temples, and gradually she stopped struggling and lay still.

She's perfect, he thought, I've never seen skin so flawless, as if she's carved out of white marble. He untangled her legs from the twisted sheet and lifted her back onto the bed, arranged her broken arm so the cast was supported by the spare pillow and bent to pick up the sheet.

'Don't go,' she said, her voice croaky and painful, her face confused and her eyes fixed on him, 'don't go away.' Then her gaze suddenly cleared, and she stared up at him. 'Where am I? What's happened?'

'You had an accident, you're in hospital in Plymouth. I'll stay here with you - don't worry, you're perfectly safe now.'

He covered her with the sheet, tucked it in at the bottom and moved his chair up next to the bed. Jamie's eyes followed his every movement, her forehead creased in confusion and then she said, 'oh, all right' and fell asleep.

He waited until he was sure she was in a deep sleep, then he rang the bell, and a nurse turned up moments later. The advantage of private hospitals, he thought, which is the same thing as the advantage of having money. He motioned for the nurse to move out into the hallway and joined her, keeping the door ajar so he could keep an eye on Jamie.

'She just had a terrible nightmare and fell out of bed, all tangled up in the sheet. She's ok, but when I lifted her back on the bed, I noticed something I want you to have a look at. I want to take a couple of photos, and I think it would be a good idea if you were in the room when I do it – in case she has another panic attack or thrashes around. It can't be good for that broken arm or her head.'

The nurse looked searchingly at him and hesitated. 'Look,' said Leo. 'I know it sounds mad, but you might have heard that the ambulance staff called the police, when she was found last night, which is how I found out that she had fallen. Well, I don't think she fell - now I think she was thrown, and the police never said anything about that to me.'

The nurse says, 'My God! What makes you think that?'

'Come and have a look.'

They went back into the room and Leo lifted the sheet and pointed silently to Jamie's lower leg. There were four oblong bruises around the ankle and above them, a rounder one slightly angled off. Jamie didn't stir when the flash went off. He waited a moment before he slowly pulled up the short sleeve of her hospital gown and there, just above her elbow was another set of bruises, four oblong marks around the outer side toward the back of her arm. He took another photo and Jamie stirred and mumbled something and Leo put his hand on hers. 'It's OK Jamie, I'm here, it's all right now', before he tucked the sheet around her shoulders again.

Back in the hallway the nurse let out a deep breath. 'Good Lord, I think you're right! Someone held her in a really tight grip - I could see how he would have done it from those finger marks. He was facing her, and he got one hand around her ankle and the other around the opposite arm. I think you're right - he lifted her and maybe he threw her. But why was he holding her by the ankle?'

'Exactly the way I see it, but the police don't know this. I talked to them earlier and they think she fell down from a fire escape on the outside of a building by accident.'

She nodded and waited, as if she could feel there was more to come.

'Perhaps she was lying down, perhaps he knocked her

over on the stairs?' The barely controlled fury he had felt since he first saw those marks nearly boiled over and he reined it in with an effort.

'I'm going to send these images to the cops. Can I have your name and phone number please? I don't know how they deal with these things, but at least I have a witness. I presume those marks weren't very noticeable when she was first examined – that they have developed since.'

'As they do. They start out red and blotchy and turn black and blue, and they often get more defined as they darken. I'm not surprised nobody noticed them before, she's got other bruises too and they had worse things to worry about.' She gave him her contact details and left.

Leo sent the photos to Grindle with a short message, then after a moment's thought he got up again, took the light rug that was folded back over the foot rail of the bed an, pulled it up to Jamie's shoulders. He moved his chair closer to the bed, left his fourth mug of coffee untouched and went to sleep in the chair with one hand on Jamie's undamaged arm.

Chapter 21

At twenty to seven in the morning the nurse came in, cast a quick glance at Jamie, who was sleeping, and said quietly, 'Inspector Grindle is here. Where do you want to talk to him?'

They stood in the hallway and Leo positioned himself so he could see in through the half open door to Jamie's room. 'Thank you – I didn't expect you to come yourself, and certainly not at this hour of the morning! I owe you twice over now.'

'I was intrigued by the photos,' said Grindle, 'and I've got to be at work at seven anyway, so I thought I'd come over and have a chat, it's more or less on my way. You must have been here all night. How bad is she?'

Leo yawned. 'Sorry! She's not too bad, I don't think – a broken arm, simple fracture and concussion and bruises.'

They looked at the photos together and Grindle watched as Leo demonstrated how he imagined someone held Jamie. 'He either held on very tight, perhaps because she was struggling, or he was lifting her. Or maybe first held her down and then lifted her to throw her.'

'Can I have a look?'

Leo hesitated for a second before he agreed. 'OK, but be quiet, don't talk while we are in the room. We don't want any more nightmares if she hears us discuss it. I know she's asleep, but still …'

He untucked the bedding at Jamie's feet and Grindle looked at her leg and nodded, then Leo showed him the bruises on her upper arm, and they retreated to the hallway.

'OK,' said Grindle. 'We'll make it an assault investigation. I checked with the station before I came here and we've got it down as a fall with a question mark, mainly because her bag was on the emergency stairs, but her phone was on the ground straight below the top landing, and no witnesses. In the absence of any other evidence, it seemed reasonable to assume she dropped her phone and leaned too far over the rail to see where it was or if it had broken. Please let me know when she wakes up so we can organize for someone to come and take a statement.'

Leo went back to his chair beside Jamie's bed and snoozed fitfully for an hour until a nurse on the morning shift came in to check on Jamie.

'I'll be in the visitors' lounge for a few minutes,' he said and left. During the night he had decided that he couldn't let Jamie go back to live in the room in the alley. It was too dangerous from several points of view; the stairs, the secluded lane and the risk her unknown assailant poses combined to make it impossible to allow her to live there. After a visit to a restroom, where he splashed his face with cold water and ran his fingers through his hair, he made three phone calls, one of them long and detailed, and finally returned to Jamie's room, satisfied that he had the situation under control.

Jamie's room had been transformed from a dimly lit scene of worry and exhaustion to a light and cheerful space. The curtains were pulled back and early sunlight cast a bright wedge of sunlight over the wall opposite her bed. She was sitting up in a freshly made bed, with her arm resting on a pillow, and her hair was newly brushed and spilled over her shoulders in thick waves of dark red. The sight of her made Leo smile when he walked in with a mug of coffee in each hand and a paper bag clutched under his arm, but Jamie frowned. He put one mug on the table beside her undamaged arm and resumed his seat beside the bed again.

'I don't get any of this! Why am I in this place?' Jamie looked as if she wasn't sure if she was angry or confused, but she needed explanations. 'It's all so weird! The nurse said this is a private hospital in Plymouth and my fiancé arranged for me to be taken here. I don't have a fiancé and I can't afford a private hospital. Is this your doing? And she said it's in my notes that you've been here all night.'

Her look challenged him, but he only said, 'Drink

your coffee while it's hot, please. I've got a sugar straw in my pocket if you want I it. And please eat one of these croissants, I got chocolate ones because you're so damn thin - you need some extra calories. You haven't been eating enough since you moved to that dreadful garret of yours, have you?'

'You haven't answered *my* questions! You should answer first,' she said crossly, but she picked up a croissant and took a bite, unable to resist it.

'Quite right, I should. Well, let me start with the most embarrassing thing, and I hope you didn't tell the nurse you don't have a fiancé, because I had to say that. You were taken to the NHS hospital, and you had no next of kin they could trace, so I wouldn't have had the authority to do anything about your situation, if I hadn't said we're engaged.'

He tried not to laugh at her outraged face. 'We don't have to remain engaged, don't panic, it's just for convenience. I didn't want you in the NHS hospital, I wanted you in a safe and comfortable place, where you can have some privacy.'

'You say, you wanted this, and you wanted that, but why? You're not responsible for me and it's going to cost a fortune and why would you even bother, and I'll never be able to pay you back.'

Suddenly she was on the verge of tears, and Leo reached out and puts his hand on hers. 'No, don't panic, I'm not trying to take your croissant. It's just as I said a minute ago – you should be somewhere nicer, and the bill comes to me, and you don't owe me anything. It was my decision, and I did it, that's all.'

Suddenly she looked vulnerable, nearly frightened. 'Do you know what happened to me? The nurse said I fell down some stairs, but I can't remember it. I was going to the supermarket, it had just got dark and I stood by the window thinking of what I was going to buy - and that's it, there's nothing more. I can't remember if I got there, or where I went after that or anything!'

Her hand twitched in his and he held it firmly, ran his thumb over her wrist and she stilled again. 'You fell from the stairs outside your room, over the railing and onto the concrete below and aside from the broken arm you've got concussion and probably a very sore patch on your head and other parts. You'll remember more later when things settle down.'

He sounds confident and calm, and she looked at him with a mixture of frustration and gratitude, and a degree of suspicion. 'Unbelievable,' she said finally. 'I can't believe you've done this for me. It feels very strange – to owe so much to someone I've been battling against for so long. And how could I possibly have fallen over the railing? It comes up as high as my elbow, I know because I knocked my funny bone several times when I carried my boxes up the stairs.'

He let her hand go and said, 'Now eat your croissant before it gets stale. And you haven't battled against me personally,' he said reasonably, and a smile softened his harsh face covered in dark stubble. 'You battled against something that you felt would harm things you value, it's not the same thing at all, not personal. And don't forget that you've done me a service that can't be measured in money, invaluable. And to some extent, I'm also the reason you lost your job and live in that room, or the Vista project is the cause.'

She took another bite of the croissant. 'Why were you here all night? The nurse said you spent the whole night in that chair and you sat there holding on to my arm for hours, she said, it's all in the notes.'

'I was making sure you wouldn't wake up scared or confused.' He drank some of his coffee and scrunched up the paper bag he had used as a plate, lobbed it in the direction of the waste-paper basket and missed.

'You had a terrible dream in the night, do you remember? It was good that I was here, because you were panicking and fell out of bed, so I moved my chair and put my hand on your arm, so I could calm you straight away, if you had another bad dream.'

She stared at him, but it was easy to see that she couldn't concentrate, she was already tired. 'Never mind, don't worry about trying to remember things, it will all come back later. Finish your coffee now and lie down and have a rest. I'm going out for a while, but I'll be back after lunch. I imagine you'd like a toothbrush and a few other things – I'll get them for you.'

He was halfway to the door before she found her voice. 'Thank you … Leo!'

And he replied, 'Don't mention it, Jamie,' over his shoulder and opened the door. That's the first time she's used my name, he thought, and then he laughed at himself.

The hallway was a bustle of early morning routines. Two nurses with trolleys of breakfast trays coming towards him glanced at him in passing, but nobody asked what he was doing there so early. Before he left, he located the administrator's office, intent on making sure nobody would bother Jamie.

'I don't want Miss Jamieson to have any visitors at all,' he said uncompromisingly to the woman, who had only just arrived to start her working day and now found herself facing a large and determined man issuing instructions. 'None! She's been bothered by a couple of people lately and it's easier to say no visitors at all, than for you to try to prevent some from seeing her or screen them on arrival or whatever. So, can you please put that in place? Preferably right now!'

The administrator was a woman in her fifties with pink streaks in her hair and scarlet nails of extraordinary length; Leo could hardly take his eyes off them, they looked dangerous.

'Of course, we can do that, but what if someone just wanders down the hall and checks all the rooms?'

She's turning this into a film script, he thought, and if she finds it too exciting, she'll gossip about it. 'I'm sure nobody would go that far.' He dragged his gaze from her nails to her face. 'She's not going to be assassinated, it's just a couple of men who have caused some problems and been a nuisance, but even that is the last thing she needs now. So please make sure nobody visits her unless I clear it.'

Should he mention that the police might come to talk to Jamie? Or would that set her off again into some drama fantasy of her own? Better not mention it. 'Thanks for your help.' He reached out to shake her hand across the desk, hoping her nails wouldn't stab him. 'I'll be back after lunch.'

It had started to drizzle again and he was glad he had taken his jacket. Before he started the car, he sent a message to Grindle: 'Please don't send anyone to talk to Jamie until after lunch. She is exhausted and needs a sleep.' He wasn't about to tell Grindle he didn't want anyone talking to her unless he was there; he planned to be back within four hours.

Chapter 22

The stairs up to Jamie's room were slippery with rain. Leo stopped on the top landing, looked down over the rail and thought of Jamie struggling with someone, then falling and hitting the ground below. He imagined her lying there, left to the chance discovery of someone passing and looking down the lane, and the picture in his mind made him wince. What if nobody had discovered her and she had lain there all night? He shook his head to dispel the thought and pulled the keys he'd taken from Jamie's bag out of his pocket.

From the doorway he looked in dismay at the dingy room. There was very little clear floor area and the beige walls and brown floor make it dark and depressing. He closed the door behind him, stopped in the centre of the room and took stock: a single bed, a small table, two upright wooden chairs and a very old chest of drawers. Along the wall a triple-height row of cartons that he presumed contain Jamie's personal possessions.

On a carton beside the bed sat a little lamp, a Kindle and its charger and an apple, and on the side of the box were two lines of writing: year 2 textbooks, assignments/term papers, photo frames, old chargers. He turned and looked closer at the long row of cartons and they too had descriptions written on the side facing out. He studied the things Jamie kept on top of the cartons; the small microwave oven, the food supplies and eating utensils. Her clothes were folded in neat piles, laid out in a row and her shoes were under the bed. A hairdryer and a small mirror on the chest of drawers, nothing in the drawers, and in the bathroom, a towel, her toiletries and a hairbrush.

Anger had smoldered since the moment he opened the door; he wanted to punch his fist hard into something. How did she get reduced to this? She moved when she lost her job, took the cheapest room she could find, and her strong sense of independence must have made her reluctant to ask anyone for help, or perhaps she didn't have anybody she felt she could ask. For a moment his outrage and pity threatened to overwhelm him. He pulled his phone out.

'Hi Derek, I'm at her place now and we don't need a truck, a van will do. Borrow the one Wilson uses, he won't be needing it during the day. And could you go and buy a suitcase on the way, please? A biggish one.'

He listened for a moment and grinned. 'No, doesn't matter if it has wheels, we've got to carry everything down a bloody fire escape. Yes, an outside one, in the rain! Find the location I sent you and park when you see my car - call me from there.'

While he waited for Derek to arrive, he sat on the bed and used his phone to reply to emails, then he made two business calls and got up again, irritated and frustrated. The room felt claustrophobic, as if the walls were closing in and he opened the door for some extra light. The damp outside air welled in and the fresh chill of the light rain brought a welcome change; his thoughts changed direction and he started to think of practical matters. What would she wear when she left the hospital – would that cast fit in a regular sleeve? There was no dressing gown in the bathroom, she was still in a hospital gown and the clothes she wore when she fell were in a paper bag in the wardrobe in her hospital room, but they would be dirty from when she lay on the wet ground and he couldn't let her put those on.

By the time Derek arrived with the van, Leo had all the boxes stacked against the wall on the dry side of the lane where the slanting rain hadn't reached.

'Start loading these, will you? And don't forget we must fit the bike in too. I'll take the suitcase up and pack the last stuff.'

No way was he letting Derek pack Jamie's clothes, or anyone else for that matter. Leo unlocked the bike and climbed the stairs again; now all that remained were the clothes he had piled on the bed, so he could move the cartons. He filled the suitcase, crammed in the coffee jar and pushed her makeup bag, hairbrush and toothbrush into his jacket pockets. The microwave oven sat abandoned on the floor with the tea towel draped over it; one last look and it was done. He locked the door and carried the suitcase down the wet stairs. It was hard to maneuver it around the right-angle turns at the two landings on the way down, but the thought of tripping and falling made him slow down.

Chapter 23

Leo arrived back at The Oaks at half past one, pleased with his morning's work and mentally planning a strategic way of telling Jamie what he had organised to, if possible, avoid making her feel that she couldn't accept his help.

He found her sitting up reading a newspaper with a lunch tray nearly untouched on the bedside table. She looked up without saying anything, studied the large carrier bag he dropped on the floor and waited for him to speak. Slightly unnerved, not a feeling he was used to, he looked back, equally serious. 'Did you tell them I'm not your fiancé?'

'No, of course not. What a silly idea.'

He raised his eyebrows. 'That's a change from this morning.'

'I only realised after you'd left what a fabulous opportunity this is,' she said coolly. 'I can sue you for breaking a promise of marriage. You've told people yourself, so it's official. I'm sure breach of promise is still on the books, there are lots of archaic laws they've never repealed. Like the one that says you can't wear a suit of armour in Parliament.'

He grinned. 'You must be feeling better. The police want to come and talk to you today. They're not happy with the idea that you fell, they think that maybe you weren't alone on the stairs.'

'What?! Why?'

He shrugged out of his wet jacket and dropped it in the corner. 'I'm not going to molest you but let me show you something.'

Gently he raised the sleeve of her gown, a blue one now, he noted, she'd had a shower and a change. Jamie stared at the bruises on her upper arm, first confused and then worried. When he moved his hand away, she puts her own hand over the marks, as if to hide them.

'And on your leg.' He pulled the covers aside and pointed to her ankle and they looked at each other for a long moment. 'Someone either held you down or lifted you – or maybe they threw you off those stairs.'

'But why?' she repeated, visibly anxious now, and he had no answer. 'I don't know, but it's got to be investigated. That's a very rudimentary nightdress they've given you. I noticed when you fell out of bed in the night that it doesn't even close up at the back, so I bought some stuff for you.' He picked up the carrier bag and put it on the end of the bed. 'Try these.' He had very nearly said, 'because I didn't want to search through your clothes', which might have ruined his chances of getting her to accept what he had done.

A few minutes later Jamie emerged from the bathroom in silky grey and pink striped pyjamas with pink satin piping around the collar. She hadn't said a single word since he handed her the carrier bag, and she went to change. Now she sat on the edge of the high bed, facing him and with her bare feet dangling just in front of him. He wanted to reach out and touch her, but of course he couldn't, he just looked at her and waited.

'Why are you doing this, Leo? All the things you bought, that gorgeous kimono and the slippers, these PJs – why?'

'It seems to me that life has been very unfair to you lately.' He had thought carefully about how to say this on the way back from his little shopping expedition. 'Your mother died, you appear to have no other family, you lost your job, and you live at the top of some dangerous stairs in a dingy room where hardly any daylight comes in. And now you have a broken arm and concussion - and we don't know how it happened.' He stopped her interrupting, as she was clearly intent on doing. 'No, let me finish. Things can't go on like this, it's not right, so I decided to do something about it, and you're not going to stay in that horrible room.'

'What!? How do you know what my room is like?'

'I went there this morning.' He met her eyes and smiled, tried to sound as if his actions were perfectly reasonable. 'I took the keys out of your bag, which the police found at the top of the stairs and brought along to the hospital, that's how they knew who you were - and the bag is in the wardrobe over there. I went to your room to pick up some things for you, but I didn't feel comfortable going through your piles of clothes or your boxes, so I bought some new things instead. Ah yes, I forgot.'

He reached for his jacket and pulled out the things from Jamie's bathroom that he had remembered to take in the last minute. 'You'll need these.' He put them on her bedside table and added her keys from his jeans pocket.

'And meanwhile you haven't had a shower or shaved or had time to change your own clothes.' She looked up at him and said seriously, 'You are the most amazing man I've ever met, there was never anyone kinder!'

'Now then, there's something we have to decide. Would you like to stay another night here? I think it might be a good idea – just in case.'

Jamie's mind snapped back to reality from the current fairytale of tempting speculations, and she couldn't believe she had not already considered this: how would she exist? Listening to Leo had swayed her grasp on reality, but now her situation came crashing back into her head and made her anxious again. She wouldn't be able to work in the bar with her arm in plaster, and they probably wouldn't have her in the restaurant either. She has no other income, so she would have to live on her savings, which were already dwindling after Bridgeman sacked her, even while she still worked at The Anchorage.

'Oh, no!' she said, visibly embarrassed. 'Of course, I

can't stay here, it's not necessary and you've already been so good to me. But I can't move, I can't afford to, so I'll go back ... I wonder if you'd be kind enough to drive me there, if you have time?'

'You're not going back to that bloody rathole,' said Leo calmly. 'You're coming home with me, to stay in the spare room, with no strings of any kind attached. I rent an apartment in Salcombe for the duration of stage one of the Visa project. Normally I live in Bath but for periods of time I need to be at the Vista site. I couldn't find a flat in Kingsbridge, so I'm in Salcombe. The apartment has a nice second bedroom with its own bathroom - very nice bathroom actually, probably better than mine.'

Her face told a story, hesitation, wistfulness and embarrassment, but he continued as if he hadn't noticed. He must get this right, so she didn't refuse. He had read her thoughts a moment ago as clearly as if they were printed on her face, and he knew he only had one moment to abort an argument.

'Your rathole room has been emptied, and all your boxes and the bike are in a van on their way to Salcombe as we speak. My assistant is a strong chap and he's going to unload everything.'

Her eyes narrowed in outrage, but before she could say anything there was a knock on the door and a nurse came in with a tray.

'You didn't eat much of your breakfast, Miss Jamieson, and I saw you had hardly touched your lunch when I came in to take you blood pressure, so I brought something that might tempt you. And I'm sure Mr Masters will join you.' The nurse cast a significant glance in Leo's direction, and he took the hint.

'Yes, please, I love scones, particularly if they have dates in them,' he said and smiled, and suddenly realised he was starving. 'Can't remember when I had one last. Do you think I could have two?'

And somehow after coffee and scones and a short sleep for Jamie, they never reverted to the issue of Leo's highhanded decision that Jamie was going to be his guest.

I'm a moral wimp, thought Jamie when she woke up from her nap. I can't resist his offer, it's too good to turn down and I truly don't know if I could bear to live in that room again, I'd be scared all the time, now that he's told me he thinks I was attacked. And I can't remember a thing, which worries me too. How would I know who it was who attacked me, and what if he comes back? He's like some kind of benevolent despot, who makes decisions and does things just because he wants to. Does he ever ask anyone if they want him to do all these things? Or is it just me, just now, because I'm hurt and he wants to help? But I have a feeling it's what he does all the time, he's got that look about him, someone called him 'decisive looking' in that article about the project, and it's true, just look at that determined chin, could be hacked out of rock.

. . .

Leo was sitting in the chair beside the bed, engrossed in something he was reading on his laptop; he hadn't noticed that she was awake, and Jamie continued to study his face without moving to alert him. He looks hard, she thought, or stern might be a better word, and that nose probably contributes to that impression. She imagined he could be a hard opponent, intimidating if he wanted to be, but he was so kind too, so generous both with his time and his money. She would have to be very careful that she didn't get too fond of him or started taking things for granted. The better she got to know him, the more attracted to him she felt, but she knew he was not for her, he was in a different league. He was often pictured in magazines and the papers with gorgeous women, all dressed up and glittering. He was used to the most and the best.

Chapter 24

Late that afternoon two police officers, one female and one male, were shown in by a nurse who looked intrigued and offered to get another couple of chairs. Jamie remained on the bed with Leo in the chair next to her.

'How are you feeling? Are you up to talking to us?' asked the female officer when they had introduced themselves. 'We're very keen to get as much detail as possible right away. Inspector Grindle saw your bruises and they could indicate that someone grabbed you and maybe pushed you or even threw you.'

Shit! thought Leo. I never told her Grindle was here and saw them while she was asleep, now I'm in for it. 'I sent Grindle photos as soon as I discovered the bruises,' he said quickly and to his relief Jamie appeared to take no notice; her attention was on the police officers.

'I don't think I'm going to be much help,' she said. 'I

can't remember anything! It's so frustrating and it worries me, it's like I can feel there are things I should be able to tell you, but I can't. I know they're there, but I can't reach them.'

'That's very common with concussions, your memory will probably return in a few days. What can you remember? You were found early yesterday evening at the bottom of the stairs outside you flat. Your bag was at the top of the stairs and your phone was on the ground, broken. Does that bring anything back?'

Jamie looked at the window with forehead ceased, as if she were looking for answers. 'I needed something for dinner,' she said slowly. 'I don't have a fridge in my … flat, so I buy something nearly every day. I remember standing by the window thinking I should take my rain jacket, because it looked as if it might rain again – and that's it. The next thing I remember is being in the ambulance.'

'Have you had any disagreement with anyone recently? Even something minor - anything that might have triggered an attack. Or have you noticed someone following you?'

The man in bar! She had apprehensive about him and Leo remembered the look of fear on her face when they got up to leave. He waited to see if she was going to bring him up. He thought of how she looked over her shoulder to see if the man was still there, how worried she had looked. At the time she had only said he stared at her, and that he seemed to always be around, that she didn't like him. But what did it mean? Did she know him, did she go out with him and then broke it off?

He waited a moment longer and when Jamie shook her head and said she couldn't think of anything, he stepped in. 'What about that guy in the bar? You said he always stares at you, and you don't like him, he frightens you.'

'Oh, him – yes, he does always stare at me. He was among those guys that confronted us at the street march. He …' She thought for a moment, while they waited to hear the end of the sentence, but she didn't continue.

'I can't remember *what* I was going to say, it was in my head and now it's gone!' She was close to tears, frustrated and worried. 'I think I'm losing my mind!'

She turned to Leo and her expression was tormented. 'Every time I push my mind to remember what happened, I feel strange, dislocated – do you think I'm going crazy?'

Leo put his hand on hers and held it tight. 'No, of course not! Don't worry about it – it will come back, I promise. Do you remember how we moved to a table where that chap couldn't look straight at you that night – he was staring at you from the bar.'

'I know what I was going to say! You've reminded me, I never told you that night – I was going to say that he's kind of aggressive while he's trying to give the impression that he likes you. He uses words like weapons, he called me 'darling' but it was like a threat. And I know what that …' Her voice tapered off and she looked as if she has lost the thread of what she was saying. 'Never mind - that's what he did at the street march. I was in the front of our group and that line of men came around the corner with a banner held in front of them and he ended up right in front of me pushing me backwards.'

The male officer looked at his colleague and they exchanged a glance. 'That's the sort of thing we mean, anything along those lines. When was the street march, and where? And was that the first time you saw him?'

'No, I'd seen him earlier that same day, in the supermarket parking lot where we all met before the march. I thought he was joining our group, that maybe he'd come with someone from Wellby. He stared straight at me all the time we were waiting for everyone to arrive, but he didn't say anything.'

'And then he turned up among the opposition? What did he say when you were face to face?'

'Something about how it was a waste that I was in the protest group and he could show me a good time – and he called me darling, but it was like a threat, I felt as if he had groped me.'

Leo clenched his jaws together to stop himself from saying something furiously inappropriate and waited.

'Let's get the details of that march,' said the woman. 'We'll see if there's any video of it online and if there is, we'll get you to point him out. Social media can be very useful, there's always someone who films what happens.' She turned to Leo. 'We need the name of the bar and the date and time. They'll have CCTV that we can have a look at.'

'Of course.' Leo was his usual calm self again and nobody would ever know about the white flame of fury that had flared in his mind when Jamie described the man she feared.

The officers left a few minutes later and Leo said casually, hoping to deflect protests. 'So, we're agreed that you'll stay here another day or two? But you can leave any time you like, it's up to you.'

'Was that inspector here, Grimmer or whatever his name was? When I was asleep or unconscious – not awake, anyway.'

'Grindle. Yes, he was.'

Jamie's face was unreadable, her eyes never left his face and she hardly blinked. 'Did you show him the bruises?'

'Jamie, I'm sorry, I should have told you. I probably went too far, but I promise you I did it for the best of reasons. I saw the bruises when I lifted you back into bed after your nightmare, and I was certain you were manhandled - either dropped or thrown, and I want the bastard caught and punished. I took photos of the bruises in the presence of a nurse and sent them to Grindle, and he called in on his way to work, very early this morning. I only showed him what he needed to see. Just your ankle and arm – he didn't see your whole body and he didn't take any photos.'

He realised how she felt, like a specimen on show, but unaware. An uncomfortable and helpless feeling, he imagined. She didn't respond, she just continued to look at him, and then suddenly she started crying. She retrieved the hand he was still absentmindedly holding and leaned forward covering her face and tears dripped between her fingers. Uncertain now, Leo got to his feet and opened his mouth to say something, but nothing came out, his mind was empty of words.

Instead, he sat down on the edge of the bed and pulled her against him, held her tight with her head tucked under his chin and Jamie relaxed into that strong, warm embrace as if the world had become a safer place. He didn't move to stroke her back, just sat there silent and solid and held her until she stopped crying.

'I wasn't really crying,' she said against his shoulder, her voice muffled. 'I *never* cry.'

'Of course, you don't – your resilience is epic. And I'm very sorry I didn't tell you earlier, I should have.'

'Don't be silly, you did what you had to do. I'm just being over-sensitive, it's probably the concussion and this constant headache.'

He let her go and she smiled a wobbly smile and then she yawned.

'I think it's nearly time for dinner, they eat very early here,' said Leo and moved back to his chair. 'I've asked them to feed me too, and I'll stay here until the visiting hours are over. It's too late now to take you home, so I'll come back tomorrow and pick you up, but if you want to stay another night, just say so.'

Long before visiting time was over Jamie fell asleep and Leo spent his time working and thinking. At nine he collected his various belongings, picked up his jacket and stood for a moment looking down at Jamie's sleeping profile. He stroked a swirl of her heavy hair away from her face, pulled the blanket up to cover her shoulders and left.

Chapter 25

Leo stopped outside a minimalist white and glass building on the steep incline above the road and got out of the car. 'Here we are. The top floor is mine for the time being.' He got her things from the back seat and nodded towards the door. 'Are you coming?'

Jamie laughed. 'I'm not planning on standing here in my PJ's and kimono - which by the way, is lovely. The local yokels will have to find someone else to stare at. But what an amazing building, it's beautiful! Does the owner live downstairs?'

'I don't think anyone lives there at the moment. That guy you recorded in the bar, his wife would have loved it. I've heard since that they looked at it after she saw it online, but he refused. And it's very expensive. There seem to be quite a few of this kind of rentals in Salcombe. The owners spend a short time here in the summers and rent them out the rest of the time. God knows where the owner of this place lives. Beijing? Singapore? Colombia?'

They went up in a lift entirely lined with bronze mirror panels and Leo grinned at Jamie's expression. 'You get used to it, but when I came home last night, I must admit I would rather not have seen six images of my unshaven face. I looked like a tramp.'

'The furniture came with the place, so it's not necessarily my taste, but it's nice enough,' he continued as he unlocked the door. They entered a large living area with a long balcony behind a glass wall and an upmarket kitchen in white tiles and stainless steel behind a dividing counter. Leo led the way to the room on the left and gestured for Jamie to go in ahead of him. 'This is the guest room.'

'Wow, are you sure it's the guest room? It looks like the master bedroom in a film star's house.'

Leo smiled. 'Who knows? I don't really care. I picked the room that gets the best direct light in the early morning, because it helps me wake up properly – mine's on the other side of the living room.'

He slid a long wardrobe door to one side and there were her boxes, neatly lined up with the descriptions of what was in them on the side facing out, and above them a dozen hangers on the rail. Leo counted the cartons and said, 'All present and correct. The clothes you had stacked on top of the boxes are in that suitcase over there on the window seat. Derek put your bike in the garage under the building, but you mustn't ride it, so I'm not going to tell you how to get in. I've got to go now, but you'll find everything you need in the kitchen and Derek's coming over to check that things are OK and ask what you want him to do.'

Before she had time to disclaim any intention to send his busy assistant running errands for her, he showed her where the intercom to the downstairs door was and left.

I can't believe how lucky I am, thought Jamie, standing in the middle of the living area with a slight feeling of unreality. He's truly the kindest person ever. And even if it's just for a short time, living here will be such a lovely respite from my life as it is right now. I'll be able to think back on this and it will cheer me up for a long time, like memories of a holiday.

She considered locating the carton with her laptop in it, but the view distracted her. When the intercom buzzed half an hour later, Jamie was sitting in the living room, still in her PJ's, dreamily watching the road that wound along the little bays towards South Sands, and the sun glittering on the waves in the estuary.

'It's Derek, Miss Jamieson, 'said the disembodied voice. 'May I come up? Mr Masters said he'd told you that I'd be coming this morning.'

'Of course - which button do I press to open the door?'

'You don't need to press anything. I've got the code and I'll be upstairs in a moment.'

No time to get dressed then, said Jamie to herself and checked her hair in the hall mirror. Never mind, I'm a convalescent, and he'll have seen a pair of PJs before, I'm sure.

Derek turned out to be a slightly overweight man in his mid-thirties with a perfect haircut and spectacles, wearing a dark grey suit with a white shirt and a dark blue tie. He's much better dressed than I've ever seen Leo, thought Jamie and smiled at the comparison.

'Miss Jamieson,' he said politely. 'I hope you're feeling a bit better. Mr Masters was quite concerned about you yesterday.'

'Yes, thanks, I'm feeling a lot better today. And thank you for bringing all my things over - it can't be the sort of thing you normally do.'

Derek smiled and his blue eyes twinkled behind the lenses. 'I do whatever Mr Masters asks me to do and sometimes that means leaving the office and doing … whatever needs doing.'

'Derek, do you call Leo, Mr Masters – to his face, I mean?'

He nodded. 'I do. He's my boss, so I do what he tells me. He frequently tells me to call him Leo, though, and it's the only order I don't obey.'

Jamie was intrigued and amused. This felt like being in an out-of-date comedy and she could see he was trying not to laugh. 'And what do *you* say when he tells you to call him Leo?'

'I say, "Yes, Mr Masters" - and then *he* says, "Watch it, Derek! One day I'll sack you for insubordination". But he doesn't mean it, I've worked for him for years.'

Jamie chuckled. The thought of Leo having met his

match was very funny, and someone as autocratic as he was deserved a secretary who wouldn't bend to his will in some detail or other.

'Perfect! What can I do for you?'

'That's my line, Miss Jamieson. I've come to show you a few things you might not have found yet and ask for instructions. And your new phone is on the kitchen bench along with the charger. Mr Masters had your broken phone, the police gave it to him, but I'm afraid the firm I took it to yesterday said it's hopelessly damaged, so I bought you a new one.'

'Derek, do you think you could possibly call me Jamie? '

'Of course, Jamie – a pleasure.' And they both laughed. This guy is gorgeous, thought Jamie, he's a treasure. 'Are you married, Derek?' she asked, though she had known nearly instantly that he was gay.

'Oh yes, I'm married to Aron, he's a dentist in Bristol - a redhead like you.'

'How long have you got? Do you want a cup of coffee – supposing there is some coffee somewhere.'

When Derek had shown Jamie where everything was kept and what was in the fridge, they sat in the living room with coffee and biscuits.

'There's plenty of choice for three or four evening meals,' he said. 'And lots of fruit in the bowl in the pantry. You need your vitamins. And I bought low-fat milk – not that you need to worry about your weight, but it seems to froth better in the espresso machine.'

'God, I hope I can cook with this damned arm! I'm right-handed, so the cast's going to be a curse.'

Derek smiled at this. 'Don't even offer! Mr Masters likes cooking, he's a very good cook. I just did the shopping yesterday, before I brought your things over, because he wanted to get back to the hospital and he knew he didn't have a lot in the fridge.'

'Nothing left for me to do,' says Jamie. 'I feel I should be doing something useful.'

'You must concentrate on getting better and resting. Oh, and your laptop is plugged in to charge,' he said, when he was leaving. 'I saw you had written on one of the boxes that the laptop was inside, so I got it out and plugged it in. It's on the wall-unit in the bedroom, I don't know if you noticed. There's note beside it with the Wifi password for the apartment. And I forgot to say, the girl in the cellphone shop said if you contact your service provider – the old one – they might be able to recover your contacts list from the cloud. I'm afraid you've got a new number, though.'

'You are a treasure, Derek! I've never in my life had anyone look after me like this – thank you! I've got my contacts list from the phone backed up on my laptop, so that's fine.'

When he left, she felt like hugging him, because he had made her laugh, but she didn't know him well enough, and it probably wouldn't fit with his secretarial ethics. He was like an old-fashioned butler or something in a film, such manners and such attention to detail, she thought, and that's probably exactly what Leo needed in his busy life. And the way he talked about Leo, with respect and affection. Probably not many powerful men had someone as genuine as Derek beside them.

She sat down on the balcony to investigate the new phone, and found two contacts already loaded, Leo and Derek. After taking a photo of the view she sent it with a text message to Leo: *Thank you for sending Derek, lovely man. I nearly proposed but he's already married. Jamie*

Getting her clothes hung up and things arranged in the bathroom took a long time. Her wrist got tired and ached when she used her right hand too much, but eventually it was done. The dry dirt came off her rain jacket after a good shake on the balcony, but the jeans she wore when she fell were filthy, so she put them in the washing machine and made a mental note to tell Leo. She took two painkillers and managed to apply mascara left-handed without any major disasters. Dressed in jeans and a favourite purple t-shirt, she made a sandwich and pulled her jacket on to sit in the sun on the balcony and eat, but a cold breeze had come up and she retreated inside.

The new phone pinged with a text alert when she was looking for her Kindle.

Glad Derek pleased you. He is my most valuable asset. I'll see you appr 6.30. Wine in rack under shelf in pantry, make sure you have a nap. Leo

Did you see my Kindle? J

Found it in my inside jacket pocket. Pile of books beside my bed, and my Kindle's there, use them. Leo

Chapter 26

Jamie hesitated to go into Leo's bedroom. It seemed like snooping, even if he had told her to do it, but the temptation to see what he read overcame her scruples.

And let's face it, she told herself, I'd love to do a bit of snooping. He's such a complex person, unreadable and emotionless expression, but kind and caring at the same time. I noticed that suppressed flash of fury yesterday when I was talking to the police, so he's got a temper, but he keeps it under control. I wonder what it was like when he confronted Bridgeman, I wish I could have seen that, I bet he was scary.

The door to his bedroom was half open, the bed was unmade and there were clothes draped over a chair in the corner. The wardrobe was open too, and all his shoes were in a jumble on the floor. Her instinct to pick up and put away, to tidy as she went, nearly won, but even as her fingers twitched, she pulled back. She had no right to touch his things, she was not his mother or his partner, or even the cleaner. On the cabinet beside the bed was a pile of books, five or six in an untidy stack and a Kindle. She flicked her finger over the button on the Kindle, read one sentence and laughed in surprise. She knew this text well, and it was the last thing she would have expected to find. He's two thirds of the way through *Pride and Prejudice*.

She took his copy of *Life after Life* from the pile of books and lay to down to read and maybe sleep. Lying on her bed she noticed a recessed shelf on the side of the bedside table, like a little cubbyhole; the only one thing in it was a foil pack of contraceptive pills. Did it belong to the beautiful black-haired girl he was with in the restaurant? She suppressed the flare of jealousy that flashed into her mind. This situation was delicately balanced. Leo was being kind, because behind that granite front, he was kinder than most, and he was grateful to her for helping prevent a major embarrassment and possibly financial loss, but she must hide how attractive she found him. That he comforted her when she cried, was probably only what he would have done with anyone who was distressed. It is just the kind of man he was and meant nothing. She felt certain that if she showed the least glimpse of being attracted, it might look as if she were taking advantage, playing the 'poor little me' game, and she would rather starve in her garret than have him think that she was trying to get something out of this strange friendship.

.   .   .

After a lunching on a banana and two crackers with cheese, Jamie sat at the round marble table with her laptop and the new phone to work out how to transfer her contacts from her laptop to the new phone. It wasn't quite the straight-forward operation she had hoped it would be, but after two attempts and some help from the Internet, she once again had the ability to contact friends by phone. Cheered by this success, which seemed to prove that her mind was still in working order, despite the persistent headache, she loaded her email account on the new phone and put it to one side. On the laptop she checked the time in Toronto; nine o'clock in the morning there and a perfect time to call Gemma on Skype, provided she hadn't got a job already.

Thank goodness for Derek, who had the forethought to give her the password for Leo's wifi, or she would have had to use the phone for all this, but the new phone had a bigger screen and would be a lot more convenient than her old one. And that was another thing she must thank Leo for. This situation was getting seriously embarrassing and reminded her of that ancient king who kept piling gifts on a beggar maid, and Jamie knew just how that girl must have felt.

'Jamie, how are you?' To see Gemma's face was such a comfort after all that had happened that Jamie felt tears come to her eyes. She had decided that she must tell Gemma everything, the whole story with all the details because trying to just mention one or two parts would end in a muddle and having to backtrack. 'Gemma, have you got time to listen to a long story or should I call back? It's a bit of a tale, it could take some time.'

'That sounds intriguing! But I've got lots of time – I haven't even started looking for a job. William is at the university most of the time, talking to his thesis supervisor and using their facilities, so I've been getting to know the city – it's a wonderful place. Huge clusters of skyscrapers and some very modern architecture, very out there, and then the old stone buildings, it's lovely. And the lake is like an ocean, much bigger than I had visualized – but the wind coming off it, you have no idea! Arctic even though it's only late autumn here. But tell me what's been going on. Where are you? I can see a very flash kitchen behind you, but I don't recognise it.'

It took an hour to tell Gemma all that had happened, and though she promised at the start to listen to the entire story and only ask questions at the end, she had interrupted a dozen times. Now she gazed at Jamie with a shocked expression. 'It sounds incredible! All that happened after we left, and I had no idea! But how are you feeling? If you got concussed only a couple of days ago, you can't possibly be fully recovered yet. And it's the second time you've hit your head, remember that you fell at the meeting in the school hall, too. You'll have to be careful now not to get any more knocks.'

'The arm will take four weeks or something, but no, I'm not recovered. I can't remember a thing about what happened. Those bruises that I showed you on my arm and leg – both Leo and the cops think I was either lifted and dropped, or maybe lifted and thrown. It drives me crazy that I can't remember. It's like someone hung a curtain across one part of my memory, I know there's something behind it, but I can't see it. And I sleep a lot, but they say my memory will come back – I do hope they're right!'

Gemma wanted to speculate on who it might be who attacked her, if that was what happened, and why, but suddenly Jamie couldn't talk about it. She was stressed and anxious again, changed the subject and diverted Gemma into talking about other things, until they ended the call.

It was strange to find that she couldn't talk to Gemma about that man. She had always been able to talk to her about absolutely anything but talking about the man from the march had nearly overwhelmed her. She had talked to Leo about it, and to the police, but that was different, and she wondered if it was because he was right there beside her, not just a face on a screen. She shied away from the thought that it could be because it was Leo, that his very presence could screen her from her from her own anxiety. The idea that her trust in him was so deep and so complete that she knew he would always protect her, always help her and never do anything to damage her, frighten her. If that's how it was, then he was irreplaceable, and she was doomed; she knew he was not for her.

· · ·

Late afternoon, after two cups of coffee and an hour reading in the living room, she took more painkillers and lay down on her bed with the book and nearly instantly fell asleep. She woke up slowly, aware of a voice nearby, a one-sided conversation. The blinds in her room had been closed and it was dusk, the room was nearly dark. She was warm and comfortable and the ache in her wrist had disappeared.

She stayed where she was, too languid to move straight away. Through the gap in the door to the living area she heard Leo talking to someone and the sound of a drawer sliding shut, the clatter of crockery.

He was cooking and talking to someone on the phone, and she wondered what he was making for dinner. She would never have guessed he would be the type to enjoy cooking, a thought that made her smile, that being big and stern faced didn't mean he had no domestic skills.

Now his voice was closer, and she imagined he had sat down at the table; he had the phone on speaker but too low for Jamie to hear the other person. He chuckled and said, 'No, why would she? I don't think she expects it to develop into love, it's about the status of being married. I think she's a practical woman, the kind who would take what's on offer and not worry about the romantic details.'

A silence and then he spoke again. 'No, I don't agree. She's not the type to make any seductive moves, she doesn't need to – sometimes proximity is enough. And of course, you're right, her position in society might possibly be one of the main drivers.'

A longer silence and then, 'OK, poppet – look after yourself.'

Jamie lay very still while her mind processed what she had just heard. My instinct was right, she thought, that feeling I had that it could easily seem suspicious, if I revealed how attracted I am to him, after never showing any sign of it before. This proves it; I must have said or done something that made him think I'm trying to take advantage, not just of his generosity, but trying to form a relationship or some kind of emotional connection – or perhaps a sexual one.

She can't think of anything in particular, but it might just be that she accepted his generous offer of help and temporary accommodation too easily, didn't protest enough. She thought back to the time he was at The Anchorage with that lovely girl with long black hair. Was that who he was talking to, or did he have several girl friends on the go at the same time? Surely someone he called 'poppet' was somebody very much younger than he was? Her mind felt strained when she tried to identify what might have given him the impression that she had ulterior and selfish motives. She failed to pinpoint anything specific and got off the bed hoping she would be able to deal with this without another headache descending on her. But she knew she was right. It would be different if she had already shown that she was drawn to him before the accident, when they met in the pub for example. But now she couldn't show the slightest sign of how she felt about him. She must keep a distance and not give anything away. The thought of him waiting for her to say or do something that proved him right made it hard to think how to cope.

'There you are!' said Leo when Jamie appeared in the doorway. 'How are you feeling? Did you have a good sleep?'

'Thanks for closing the blind, that was kind of you. I had a long sleep.' She stood indecisive just inside the room and he pulled out a chair at the table. 'Come and sit down – dinner will be ready in five minutes. I was just about to wake you up. Would you like a glass of wine?'

Leo was worried about how unwell she seemed. He had expected that when she woke up, they would talk about what she had done during the day, but now there seemed to be a barrier between them, he felt it like a physical presence. Was it of her making, or was it her unwellness? Her texts earlier in the day had seemed energetic and lighthearted, much livelier than she had been in the hospital, but now she looked troubled and confused. He hoped it was because she had just woken up and not the concussion creating lasting problems.

Over dinner she became progressively more subdued until by the end of the meal she hardly looked up from her plate. 'That was delicious – thank you for cooking for me.' She puts her knife and fork down. 'I don't think I should finish my glass of wine. I don't feel quite well – I think I'll go to bed.'

Leo tried to make up his mind whether the best option was to ask what was wrong or leave it until the morning. He could sense an unease and a restraint that he thought they had left behind them. Was his feeling that she had come to trust and like him just wishful thinking? He wished her a good night's sleep and when the door closed behind her, he felt she had shut him out.

Chapter 27

Jamie's dream started and stopped and started again. She locked the door to her room and turned around to go down the stairs, she locked the door and turned around to go down the stairs and there was a man on the landing below her and he was coming up towards her. He smiled and she knew who he was, and he said, 'hi darling, you and I are overdue for some fun – I think you owe me' and the menace behind his smile told her everything, he was going to harm her. She turned and tried to get the key out of her bag to unlock the door, but he took three quick steps up and reached for her ankle, just managed to get his hand around it. She screamed 'let me go' but she couldn't reach the door. She grabbed the handrail and hung on desperately as he tried to pull her down towards him. He had lost his footing, the whole iron structure was shaking, and now he was kneeling on the stairs just below her feet. He yanked hard and she knew her fingers were about to let go, her mind said, let him do it, let him rape you, don't fight, he's too strong. But the horror of being alone with him in her room, where nobody could hear her, gave her new determination. She focused her entire strength on the hand holding on to the rail and gritted her teeth. Now he was on his feet again, still holding her by the ankle, and he lifted her leg up high, she had to let go of the rail, her shoulder hit the top step hard, but she kicked at him with her other foot. He took hold of her upper arm and lifted her, but she twisted in his grip and suddenly she was falling, turning in the air as the ground came up towards her, and she screamed.

She was awake now, but the terror was still with her, like a cold weight in her chest, she could hardly breathe. She knew where she was and that she was safe, but she couldn't stop trembling. And then Leo was beside her, sat down on the bed and pulled her towards him, wrapped his arms around her. 'It's OK Jamie, it's me − it was a dream. It's over, you're OK.' He continued to talk in a low voice and held her tight against his chest and gradually her breathing settled down and she stopped trembling. She realised that her cheek was against his bare chest, she heard his heartbeat, strong and even.

'Sorry, it was a dream.'

'I know, you screamed. Do you want to tell me about it?'

'That man, the man from the street march, he came to get me, and he was going to force me to go back inside. I was on the top landing and I'd locked the door.' She drew a shaky breath. 'He was going to rape me, in my room, he said I was going to enjoy it. He called me "darling" and he smiled.' She shuddered at the memory.

'And what happened then?'

She described the struggle and how she fell. 'But it happened so fast - I don't know how I went over the rail.'

'But he lifted you and when you struggled, you went over?'

She considered for a moment, tried to remember the dream and wondered if it *was* the dream she was describing, or if she now remembered what really happened.

'I don't think he threw me, but it was so quick, there was no time to think. And I don't know if my dream is exactly like what happened in reality, anyway. I don't even know if what I told you is the dream or my memory, it might be both.'

'But when you think back now, when you're completely awake, does it feel like reality? And you're sure of who it was?'

'Oh yes, it was the man who was in the bar that night, I'm absolutely sure of that, it's not just what was in the dream.'

And not until then did she realise that Leo was still holding her, and she was still leaning against him. She moved and he let her go and got up from the bed. She slid down under the covers and watched as he pulled the door nearly shut behind him. It was dark outside and she couldn't be bothered checking what the time was. She lay still, feeling unsafe even there, as if the man might find her, as if he might still be looking for her, wanting to harm her.

What was she going to do when she left here? And leave she must, she couldn't possibly stay here after what she overheard before dinner. She felt as shamed as she would have been if those speculations were true. Her mind transformed what she heard into a kind of truth, even though she knew her motives were not those he voiced in that phone conversation. But contrary to her expectation of a sleepless night, she fell asleep, then the dream started again.

… she locks the door to her room and turns to start down the stairs and suddenly a man is on the landing below her, and he is coming up towards her. He smiles and she knows who he is, he says, 'hi darling, you and I are overdue for some fun – I think you owe me' and she tries to quickly get the key out of her bag … she screams "nooo!"

Leo was in her room seconds later, put his hands on her upper arms and tried to hold her still, but she struggled in his grip, caught in the terror of her dream. The pillow was on the floor, the sheet was tangled around her, and she was in a strange state, halfway to awake. He couldn't seem to wake her properly, he said, 'Jamie, it's me, wake up', but she continued to struggle. Her eyes were open, but without focus, and he knew she couldn't see him. He let go of her arms, walked quickly around the bed and got in behind her. Ignoring her twisting body and flailing arms, he put his left arm over her body and took hold of her undamaged left wrist. Her legs were kicking, she cried out, 'let me go, let me go' and he put his leg over hers, and pulled her back against his chest. Now she was still, securely anchored and she stopped struggling. He murmured words of comfort, a meaningless stream of short phrases and gradually she relaxed more and more until her breathing told him she was deep in normal sleep.

Lying absolutely still, Jamie tried to work out where she was, and who was in bed with her. Gradually things sorted themselves out in her mind: she was in Leo's apartment in Salcombe and for some reason he was in her bed. His arm was across her body and his hand held her left wrist. It was very early morning; she could see muted light through the curtains. Dawn, she thought, but how long had he been there and why? She managed to raise her plaster cast arm enough for her right hand to reach his hand that held her wrist; she pulled his fingers away.

'Sorry,' he said behind her and let her wrist go. 'Did you get scared?'

She turned over, and he grabbed her right arm before the cast hit him in the face. 'Careful!'

Now that she had turned over, she realised how close he was, very close. He lowered her arm and rested the cast on his hip, and she felt suddenly anxious, her voice trembled. 'What happened, why are you in my bed? I can't remember … what did we do? I think I am losing my mind.'

He put his arm over her again and rocked her a little, she felt his warm breath on her forehead and his palm flat against her back. 'Don't worry – you're not losing your mind, I promise. You had a nightmare again, a second time. Do you remember the first one, when you screamed, and I came in and you told me who had attacked you?'

'Oh yes, of course! You came in and woke me, and we talked about it. But didn't you leave? I thought you went back to your room.'

'I did, and then just before dawn, can't be more than half an hour ago, you had the same nightmare again, or something very like it. And I couldn't wake you – you were kind of half-awake and thrashing around like a wild child, arms flailing, legs kicking. I was worried that if I forced you awake you would panic even more, so I got in behind you and sort of anchored you to the bed, and you went to sleep.'

She lay still, silent and frightened. Why couldn't she remember this? Why couldn't he wake her up?

'There must be something wrong with my brain!' she said on the verge of tears, and she could hear how scared she sounded. 'Not being able to wake up – it isn't normal!'

His arm tightened around her, and he kissed her forehead; his lips were warm and comforting. 'Please don't worry – you're concussed, and you're traumatized by the attack and it's all too much to cope with.' He bent his head and puts his cheek against hers and somehow the feel of his stubble grazing her skin was a comfort in the midst of her confusion.

'I think the nightmares will go on for some time, and then all this will fade, and you'll be all right again.' His voice was calm and confident, he didn't sound as if he was making it up to comfort her. His hand cradled the back of her head, pulled her face against his neck and everything about him was warm and solid. Without any thought she put her mouth against his neck and whispered, 'thank you' and felt his body instantly react. His hand moved and he raised her chin and then his mouth was on hers, he kissed her in a way she had never been kissed before. He parted her lips and kisses the inner edge of her bottom lip as if he was marking a boundary. Her breath quickened and she put her hand on his cheek. His eyes looked into hers and she knew it was too late to pretend she wasn't attracted to him, to pretend she didn't want him to make love to her. He was kissing her neck and she knew it's too late to stop now, she desired him in a way she had never desired anyone before. He rolled her onto her back and his warm hands were on her shoulders, running down her upper arms, then cupping her breasts.

'Jamie,' he said, his voice sounded like a growl from deep inside him. 'If we don't stop now, I won't be able to.'

And she whispered, 'Oh, please don't stop!'

Chapter 28

Jamie woke up slowly, alone but snug and warm, and realised the covers had been tucked in all around her; she was in a warm cocoon. Lying perfectly still she remembered their love making, the feel of his hands on her body, his lips on her skin. And out of nowhere the memory of the conversation she overheard yesterday sprang back into her head and she groaned with frustration. Would he think of this as confirmation that she was trying to entrap him somehow, that she had ulterior motives? Or would he understand that genuine and spontaneous feeling underpinned what happened? But wasn't this exactly what he was talking about yesterday? That she might be in it for financial security, that it wasn't love, that proximity was enough to form a connection. She couldn't bear for him to think she had proved what he suspected, and nearly anything she did now would confirm it in his mind, it made her cringe just to think about it. She had made a mistake with a man once before and it turned into a disaster, an uneven, depleting relationship where she was always on the back foot, forever trying to prove impossible things. In the end, it sucked all her self-confidence out of her, and she swore she would never make another mistake like that - it would destroy her.

When she heard noises from the living room she rose, put the kimono on and joined him in the living area.

'I've made toast,' said Leo from the open plan kitchen, and he sounded so normal, as if nothing happened. 'Come over here and help yourself, I'm just making coffee.'

She didn't know how to act with him now, she was uncertain of what would be the right move, so she simply walked across to the kitchen, buttered a slice of toast and carried it to the table. She simply couldn't think of anything to say that wasn't going to either feed into his belief she was manipulating him or leave herself more vulnerable than she was already. And she had no idea what he was thinking. His face was unreadable, and he sounded so ordinary, talking about coffee. Maybe the sex was just a casual urge, something without meaning, just one body interacting with another. So, over breakfast they both read things online, spoke little and all the while Jamie was as tense as a steel spring. She wanted to say something about it, but she failed to find the right words and then realised she had left it too late.

Leo took his cup and plate to the kitchen and said, 'I've got to leave early today, it's going to be a busy day. I asked Derek to load his number on your phone, so please call him if you need anything. I've got two meetings in Bath, and I'll be late back, but just help yourself to whatever you like, don't worry about me – I'll make something quick when I get home.'

He paused just before opening the door to leave, turned and looked straight at her, very serious. 'Jamie, if you have a sleep during the day and have that dream again, call me! I'll take the call, I promise, and we'll talk about it. Please, don't try to deal with it alone.'

As Leo drove away from Salcombe he was mired in contradictory emotions. I shouldn't have done that, he thought, I've been wanting to for so long, ever since I saw her in the lawyer's office, I think. There's something utterly captivating about her, something apart from her looks – it might be the way her spirit shines through everything she says and does. But she's in a vulnerable situation right now and I should have stopped. It was unforgivable – as if I was implying that she had to pay me back for looking after her. But it was marvellous, incredible - and she enjoyed it too, I know she did. I wonder what she was thinking, she was so subdued again this morning. Somehow, I couldn't think of a way to bring it up and then I left it too late.

Halfway to the Vista site he suddenly realised that he couldn't remember taking his phone. He patted his pockets and found nothing. 'Bugger!' he said out loud, but there wasn't enough time to turn around to get it. He had only just enough time to go to the Vista site, pick up the papers Derek would have ready for him and continue straight to the Bath office for the meetings.

'Derek,' said Leo hurriedly, as he walked into the portable site office. 'I was late leaving, and I've left my phone behind. Can you please call Miss Jamieson and ask her to find my phone and keep it handy? Tell her she can answer it if she wants to and take a message to relay to you, or she can just tell you who called – it will show on the screen. I suspect these damn meetings will take a while, so I might not see you until tomorrow. Are those the papers I need?'

He took the folder and went straight out to his car, did a U-turn and disappeared towards the gates. Derek looked thoughtfully after him, straightened the papers Leo had pushed sideways and picked up his phone.

'Good morning, Jamie – it's Derek. How are you?'

'I'm fine, thanks.' She could hear that her voice was dull, but it was too late now to try to change the tone.

'I'm calling to say that Mr Masters left his phone behind somewhere in the flat. Could you find it please and keep it where you can hear it, and if someone calls him, just take the call and give them my number, so I can deal with whatever it is or else just text me and tell me who called. Text messages will show on the screen too, so you can text me and tell me who it was. I think that's all.'

They talked about nothing much for a few moments and then Derek was interrupted by someone coming into his office, and he said goodbye.

Jamie found the phone on the bench in the kitchen, put it on the table and went to get dressed. She would like to talk to someone and hesitated between her old friend Louisa and Gemma, but Louisa would be on her way to work and it wasn't even morning in Toronto. And maybe she shouldn't mention this to anyone, maybe everyone would assume she was an opportunist, out for what she could get. She didn't think Louisa would, but would Gemma maybe think that?

Undecided about what to do, Jamie stood at the glass wall in the living room and looked across the road to the estuary, where the water was grey instead of blue today and ruffled by angry little waves. Two women were walking towards the entrance downstairs, and she wondered vaguely what they are doing. Wasn't the ground-floor apartment empty? Behind her Leo's phone pinged, and on the screen was a that Trapido Transport had sent a message. She called Derek to tell him, but his phone was busy, and while she was leaving him a message the door phone buzzed, and she jumped. Who could possibly come calling this early in the morning? She pressed the button with a camera image and when the little screen lit up, she saw a slightly distorted image of Prissy and Harriet. 'Jamie, darling! You poor girl, can we come up?'

They breezed into the living room like a human tornado, carrying a bunch of flowers and a huge box of chocolates and talking over each other. Jamie was hugged and kissed and exclaimed over and it took several minutes for her to make herself heard.

'Heavens, you two – what a surprise! What lovely flowers, thank you! We'll have to find a vase.'

'Bound to be one in the kitchen,' said Harriet and started opening cupboards. 'Hey, look Prissy! He's got those gorgeous wine glasses we at looked at in London, remember how you lusted after them – they cost a bomb, Swedish crystal.'

Prissy crowded in to look over Harriet's shoulder and while they were talking about wine glasses and if they really were the same as the ones they saw in Harrods, and whether they belong to the landlord or Leo, Jamie quietly found a vase and put the flowers in water. When they finally sat around the marble table with coffee and chocolates, Jamie looked affectionately at them. 'You two are incredible! I can't believe you found me. How on earth did you know where I was?'

'Easy cheesy,' said Harriet. 'First Prissy heard about the accident from her brother's girlfriend who's a paramedic. They came for dinner at Prissy's place last night, and she put two and two together. And she told me first thing this morning, so I called the hospital in Plymouth, because we knew they took you there. Then we found out you'd been moved to The Oaks, so I called The Oaks and told the admin person there that I'm your cousin – you know how they refuse to tell you things these days if you just say you're a friend? And she said you'd been discharged.'

'But how did you find out I was here?'

'Aha! You don't know how it works here, you're far too new and anyway I think you have to be born here or at least it takes years and years to become part of the network.'

'True,' said Prissy. 'I live in Kingsbridge, so I don't count as a local and nobody from here would tell me a thing!'

'Apart from me! Anyway,' continued Harriet, 'I live in South Sands, and we've been there for so many years we count as locals now, and people tell us things. And the chap who runs the dinghy hire told me when I took the dogs for a walk this morning. He said he was driving past yesterday morning and he saw Leo Masters standing outside this place with a girl with red hair dressed only in her PJs. Which of course was enough to attract anyone's attention, even the boatman. I mean, a girl in her PJs arriving with Leo Masters? And everyone is interested in what Leo Masters does anyway - he's such a fascinating man. I love a good-looking, brooding hunk of a man, myself and he's the perfect specimen.'

'But why are you staying with *him*?' asked Prissy. 'I would have thought he would hate the look of you after all the hassle your lot caused him. And you must tell us how you got hurt! And how did he find that out, anyway? Or have you two suddenly got a thing going? Like hating each other and then realising you love each other, like some tacky romance?'

'No, no — of course we don't! I hardly know him,' said Jamie quickly and lifted the lid on the box of chocolates as a distraction. The memory of Leo in her bed and his hands on her body had flashed into her mind and made her feel overheated. 'Have a chocolate! It was just that I did him a favour, or rather I did a favour for his company, I found out about a fraud that was being planned, so I told him. It's in the hands of the police now. And then when my accident happened, the police officer he had talked to about the fraud called him – he thought we were old friends, you see. And Leo turned up at the hospital and did his total autocratic thing, took over, told them he was my fiancé, so they wouldn't protest, had me moved and made all kinds of decisions. And all the while I was sedated and knew nothing about it! And then I woke up in a luxury room in a private hospital and had no idea how I got there.'

With interruptions and questions, it took a good while to go over the whole story. Harriet and Prissy wanted every detail explained; from the attack on the fire escape and who her attacker was to why she had been living in a room above a factory.

They insisted on finding out how she knew about the fraud, so she told them how she overheard something in The Anchorage bar, recorded it and passed it on to Leo, and that he had reported it to the police. Everything had to be told again and exclaimed over and commented on.

Prissy tried to squeeze more details from Jamie about what she heard in the bar, but she resisted. 'No, I can't talk about it. The police asked me to keep it to myself while they investigate.' God forbid, she thought, if these two found out the details, the whole world would know by tomorrow morning.

Prissy's eyes had roved around the living room while

she listened to Jamie, now she pointed to Leo's bedroom door which was half open.

'Is that his bedroom? Have you been in there?' Pushing her chair back, she was about to get to her feet, and Jamie said quickly, 'Of course I haven't been in his bedroom!' and Prissy grinned. 'But wouldn't it be fun? I wonder what he reads – and is he tidy?'

'Not that I don't want to go and have a peep myself,' said Harriet and looked longingly at the half-open door, 'but we really shouldn't, Prissy. I know we often behave badly, but that would be a step too far.' She held up her hand. 'Yes, I know what you're about to remind me of, and yes, we did have a look in Clare's wardrobe that night when we went upstairs to the bathroom, but this is Jamie's safe haven, we mustn't do it.'

Prissy sat back again and Jamie said, only half in jest, 'I wouldn't be surprised if this flat is covered by CCTV, he's super careful with things like that. The perimeter fence out at the Vista site has cameras and lights at intervals and I bet they check them all the time – on the lookout for dangerous protesters like me.'

'I had an email from Gemma this morning,' said Harriet and picked out another chocolate. 'Did she tell you, when you Skyped, that those people who rented their house are leaving already? They contacted her and said their plans have changed and they are moving out more or less straight away. She's furious, because now she must find new tenants – and she was so pleased to have found that couple for a whole year. You could live in her house, Jamie, it's the perfect solution!'

Jamie knew she couldn't, but she wasn't prepared to go into details. She couldn't afford Gemma and William's house, and they needed the rent from it. That Prissy or Harriet would talk to Gemma about letting the house to her was probably one hundred percent likely, so she must lie about where she was going to live when she left Leo's place – before they asked. She certainly didn't want Gemma feeling guilty that she couldn't offer Jamie the house.

Aloud she said, 'What a strange thing, leaving so soon when they leased it for a year! But I'm going back to Bristol at the weekend to stay with my friend, Louisa – her flat mate has left. Why are those tenants leaving so suddenly?'

And then it struck her that she already knew, she just hadn't put the pieces together or maybe she had forgotten. Of course, she thought, Leo said he was firing the man I recorded in the bar, and Gemma's tenants are the daughter and son-in-law of William's colleague, and Leo thought I would know 'the man's father-in-law' because he thought I worked at the law office. My mind just isn't up to speed yet, I need more RAM.

'Apparently, he got a job offer he couldn't resist, so he resigned and they're leaving immediately. But tell me, Jamie,' says Harriet. 'What's it like staying with Leo? I've only met him socially a couple of times, but he's so intriguing! Prissy is quite besotted, she says he's like Heathcliff and Mr Darcy rolled into one.'

Prissy laughed and punched Harriet in the upper arm. 'You're such a fibber, darling – it's not just me who thinks he's fabulous, you do too! And probably every other female, who has ever seen him, not to mention some guys. You know that irresistible mix of the hard-faced man with a great body and lots and lots of money – and power! Who could resist it?' She pulled the chocolate box away from Harriet and repositioned it between Jamie and herself. 'Enough of those, you'll start moaning about your weight again and you've just spent weeks starving yourself. And what *is* Leo like at home, Jamie? I've never met a tycoon type person in their own house, rich people, yes – tycoon, no.'

'He is kind and generous, and very calm.' She thought for a moment. 'He enjoys cooking, and he reads books.'

'Really? Who would have thought? Too good to be true.' Harriet laughed. 'You should grab him quickly before that Lucinda woman does. They've been together on and off for years and she's not getting any younger, she'll be desperate to hook him for life.'

'Rubbish!' interrupted Prissy. 'He'll never marry her, and she doesn't need his money anyway, she's got plenty of her own. I bet you a hundred he'll marry someone young and gorgeous, if he ever marries at all.'

'Who is Lucinda?'

'Lucinda Webber-Smith – former model. She lives in a penthouse in London, she was the second highest paid model in the world about ten years ago, perhaps a bit longer. She seems to spend most of her time in nightclubs and on yachts these days with other famous people. Still gorgeous, but rumour has it she's a real bitch. Her modelling name, or whatever they call it, was 'Sinda' with an S– remember her?'

'Oh yes, I do - she was stunning and about ten feet tall. Of course, I remember her! When I was twelve or thirteen, I used to think she was the ultimate ideal woman.'

'You're so young, I forgot! You must be at least ten years younger than us – lucky thing!' Prissy unwrapped another chocolate, and Harriet snatched it out of her fingers just as she was about to put it in her mouth, they both laughed, and Jamie smiled and had another chocolate herself.

The process of saying goodbye took fifteen minutes and even after they were outside, she could hear them talking as they walked to their cars. They were so kind and so funny, but they made her feel exhausted, they never stopped talking and laughing and interrupting each other, and obviously neither of them needed to work. How different their lives were from her own.

Chapter 29

Jamie was putting the cups in the dishwasher when Leo's phone made a buzzing sound. She picked it up and saw that someone with the initials LWS was calling and took the call.

'This is Leo Masters' phone. Can I help you?'

'I want to speak to Leo,' said a woman, who was clearly used to being obeyed. 'And why is he not answering his own phone? Who are you?'

'Mr Masters is in a meeting in Bath and he left without his phone. Can I take a message?'

The demanding woman at the other end was not happy with this response. 'Why doesn't Derek answer his phone then?'

God! thought Jamie, what is this, the inquisition or something? 'He left the phone at his apartment,' she said patiently. 'I can pass a message on to Derek or I can give you Derek's number, if you want to speak to him.'

'I don't want to speak to Derek! I want to speak to

you. What the fuck are you doing in Leo's flat? And who are you? I know he's got some girl staying there, I suppose you're some little slut he picked up in a bar. Well, don't get any ideas! I bet you know what a catch he is, and you've got your eye on the main chance, but it won't work – he's not for some little scrubber like you.'

Jamie was so taken aback she couldn't think of a reply for a moment. She nearly ended the call, but the woman's rudeness made her want to hit back. 'I have no idea who you are,' she said and hoped she sounded calm. 'And I don't know why you think it's any of your business if I'm staying here.'

'I bet you played the poor little girl card. I hear you have your arm in plaster. Bet it was easy to trick Leo into letting you come and stay – that man's too damn kind for his own good. Well, you'd better get out smartly, he's not for someone like you and you're wasting your time. Crawl back into your gutter or wherever you came from and stay there, or I'll come down and throw you out.'

She's drunk, thought Jamie, it's way before lunch and she's drunk. Wonder if she was up all night, drinking? And she must have some friend down here who heard about me – this is so rude!

And in the back of Jamie's mind a great idea appeared as if from nowhere while she listened to this tirade. 'Are you Emily or are you Poppet?' she asked. 'I bet you're Emily! Did you leave your contraceptive pills here? I found them in the bedroom yesterday.' She deliberately didn't say which bedroom. Let her stew, she thought, she deserves it.

'Who the hell is Emily? I never heard of her. I'm Sinda, and Leo belongs to me.'

Jamie managed to produce a small chuckle, though it nearly choked her. 'Aha, that's who you are, Leo has talked about you. So, the pills won't be yours then, you're too old to need them. Sorry, it was nice to talk to you, but I've got to go now.'

When she put the phone down after this ordeal, her hand was shaking. Confrontations upset her more than she would ever admit to anyone and now she felt physically sick. I really should be able to conquer this, she told herself, it's five years ago and I did leave on my own initiative, nobody had to rescue me, apart from Louisa picking me up in her car. I keep thinking I'm OK, but then some stress situation brings it all back and turns me to a quivering wreck. Pathetic!

Jamie closed her eyes and replayed the conversation with Sinda and then the one she overheard Leo having with someone he called 'poppet'. Not her, thought Jamie, Lucinda wasn't the kind of woman you call poppet, too old and too tall. I'm quite proud of myself for inventing Emily and remembering the pills! I'm not usually good at this sort of thing, I mostly only think of the perfect reply when it's way too late.

Sitting in the living room Jamie stared out the window without focus and tried to work out what to do. Now she didn't notice the view over the water, her entire focus is inwards. Staying here had become impossible; she was trading on Leo's generosity and kindness. His primary woman friend regarded her as a slut and an intruder in his life, and he had discussed her possible motives with the unknown Poppet, quite explicitly and calmly, with a laugh hidden under his voice, as if he found the situation amusing. She had nowhere to go, no local friends she could ask, and she couldn't ride her bike with her arm in plaster. Well, she probably could, but she couldn't get into the garage.

She would leave, take only what she needed and catch the bus to Kingsbridge. Briefly she considered asking Harriet or Prissy if she could stay with one of them, but her sense of self-preservation told her that she might lay herself open to more criticism, and she would be taking advantage of yet another person, who wasn't even a friend of long standing. She would find somewhere cheap, use her savings until she found a job, anything that she could do to earn a little money.

Her thoughts turned to practical plans. She didn't need a lot, just a simple place to stay and a job that paid enough for basic things until the cast came off and she could get a proper job. She would re-establish herself somewhere and when the car insurance payout arrived, she would reimburse Leo for the phone and then later, she would move back to Bristol and restart her normal life. Going back to Bristol right away was the obvious solution, but some unidentifiable emotion stopped her even considering it, as if doing that would mean too definitive a break.

The suitcase Leo had packed her clothes into was far

too big and she doubted that she could carry a full suitcase if she had to walk a distance, not with one arm in a cast and unable to change hands. Rummaging among Leo's belongings felt like invading his privacy but finding something to pack in was a must. In a hall cupboard she found a sports bag, medium sized and with a shoulder strap. She would take nothing heavy, just what she absolutely needed and then she'd ask Leo to forward the rest when she had found somewhere to live. She packed underwear and socks, a spare pair of jeans, three tops, her new PJs and a pair of shoes. In the last moment she folded the kimono and put it in the bag, stroked the silky surface and felt tears pool in her eyes.

The bag was now full and the laptop wouldn't fit, but it was extra weight and she couldn't use it anyway, not until she was somewhere with access to wifi. She put the phone charger in the bag and pushed her toilet bag and makeup in after it; now she could only just zip the bag up and it was heavier than she had anticipated.

With the bag waiting beside the front door, she sat down at the table with her laptop to search the Internet on a big screen while she had the opportunity. First accommodation and then jobs, and gradually her list grew. She would make calls from the bus or when she arrived in Kingsbridge and surely, she would find something; there must be a room and a job in one of the towns in the region.

With the list finished, she put the laptop on the shelf in the bedroom and by the time she left, her bedroom was tidy, and the bed was stripped. With some difficulty she folded the sheets and put them on the end of the bed. It took an inordinately long time to compose a note to Leo on a sheet of paper she took out of the printer on the sideboard, but finally it was done, and she put it in on the table beside the flowers that Harriet and Prissy brought. She left Leo's phone beside the note and stood looking down at it for a long moment, then she touched it gently one last time with her fingertips, aware that she was about to makes an irreversible break.

She had an apple, a banana and a ham sandwich in the big square pockets of the black jacket, and in the last moment she took a handful of chocolates out of the box Prissy and Harriet had brought and stuffed them in after the banana. When Jamie let the door fall shut behind her, with one move she was back in the desolate world of hardship and worry.

A woman who passed on a bike pointed the way to the bus stop where she waited for an hour, glad of the black jacket now that the wind from the estuary was getting stronger. Under she shelter of the little roof she pulled out her phone and started calling possible landlords, but by the time the bus arrived she had not had any luck. On the bus she continued calling and ticking off items on the list and realised she might have to consider extending her search to Exeter. Kingsbridge had B&B rooms available at this end of the season, but landlords still expected rent at a level she wasn't prepared to pay; she must make her savings last and moving further away was a safer option anyway. The thought of meeting her attacker again made her feel sick with fear. She knew he might not just have raped her, he might have killed her, so moving on was the safe idea and there was nothing to keep her in Kingsbridge, now that Heather had died dead, and Gemma was in Canada. Her headache got increasingly worse to the point where she considered trying to swallow a couple of painkillers without water, but the prospect of choking and possibly vomiting on the bus stopped her.

In Kingsbridge Jamie went straight to the nearest café, not the one that belonged to Sue, because she was reluctant to talk to anyone about what had happened and why she was in this situation. As the afternoon progressed Jamie tried to think of where she could stay that night without spending too much but still be safe. The thought of having to pay full price for a room was daunting; until the insurance company finally paid for the loss of the car, her savings were her lifeline. She plugged her phone into a wall socket just beside her table and called one number after the other until she struck it lucky not long before the café was closing at four.

'I didn't know the ad was still there, I let that room last year, but I do have another room, much smaller,' said an old man in Torquay, whose advertisement she made a note of that morning when she was using the laptop. 'It's not very good and I've never let it before, and it's only the size of a biggish bathroom, really, I don't know what it was originally. The house is two hundred and fifty years old and my wife used to say it was probably the maid's room, it's beside the kitchen. You can have it any time you like, but you'd better come and inspect it first, before you decide - it's nothing grand, so I wouldn't charge much.'

She told him she would be there the next day and call him when she got off the bus. When the café closed, she walked to Gemma and William's house in a chilly breeze and studied the house from the opposite side of the street. There was no car outside and she knew the garage was full of things Gemma packed up before they left, so maybe the house was empty. Better to take the chance now, she thought, rather than wait until dark. If the tenants hadn't left, she would have to make some excuse, and the risk of some neighbour reacting now while it is still light was probably minimal, but after dark it might look more suspicious.

She crossed the street, walked up the short driveway, along the path to the corner of the house and into the garden at the back. The garden looked different now than it did on that late summer day when Gemma and William had their big dinner party. Now leaves were falling from some of the trees, the plum tree in particular looked tired with hardly any leaves left, and the sight of it made Jamie feel melancholy, as if nature was conspiring to sadden her. In the corner by the terrace the roses looked as if they were ready to give up, begging to be pruned.

Jamie remembered helping Gemma summer-prune them in early July after the first intensive blossoming was over, and Gemma saying, 'If I ever get married again, I'll be married in June and have the church full of scented roses.' And Jamie had smiled and replied, 'If you ever get married again, I hope you marry William.'

In the far corner of the garden was a shed-cum-workshop and in her mind, she could hear Gemma's voice saying, 'We need the wheelbarrow – I'll get it out now. We keep a spare key out here, so we don't have to go inside when we want something.'

Jamie reached up to the hook under the eaves on the side of the shed that was up against the hedge and found the key, unlocked the door and went inside. The shed felt warm and dry and after a moment's thought she locked the door from the inside.

Just in case the tenants were still living in the house she didn't turn the light on and wondered if even the screen on her phone might make a glow they would notice through the window, now that dusk was falling. She pulled the folded plastic tarpaulin from the shelf above the lawnmower and arranged it with some difficulty into a long narrow shape under the workbench, creating a make-shift bed. Sitting on an upturned bucket she waited for darkness to fall. There was no sound from the house or the garden and every now and then she got up and looked out the window, but no lights came on in the house.

Time dragged, she counted to a thousand, then she did it again, until she finally crawled in under the bench and turned the phone on. It was half past seven now and she had a missed call notification, a voice message, two text messages and an email, but she checked none of them and turned the phone off. Now she needed to pee, but she was reluctant to leave the safety of the shed, and squatting in the garden in the dark was not an appealing idea, so she used the bucket and remembered her mother saying, 'Needs must, darling' whenever anything seemed unpleasant. Then she plugged the phone in to charge on the shelf where William kept his power tools and lay down under the workbench with her spare jeans folded under her head hoping to get some sleep.

Possibly this is an over-reaction, she thought and tried to find a comfortable way to support the cast on her arm, but if I have to spend the night in Kingsbridge, it's nice to be somewhere I feel safe - and it's free. Tomorrow I'll move on. The thought stabbed her heart like a knife: moving on, moving away.

Chapter 30

Still with his satchel slung over his shoulder, Leo stood by the table and read Jamie's note a second time, then he said 'fuck!' very quietly, dropped the bag on the floor and sat down to read it a third time.

Dear Leo

Thank you for your kindness and generosity, which have meant more to me than I can express. I have become aware that staying here could be seen as an attempt on my part to try to create a 'situation' or a 'connection' with you, maybe to entice you into a sexual relationship for personal gain or advantage. I know you were kind because I had helped you, when I recorded those men in the bar, but the rest of the world doesn't know this. I left my boxes in the wardrobe and I will arrange for them to be picked up when I have a place to stay and the means to do so. If they are in the way you could perhaps put them in your garage? I took a bag from your hall cupboard, sorry! But I'll return it eventually. I took the phone as I have no other means of communicating, but as soon as I find a job, I will reimburse you for it. Can you please let the police know that I now remember the man who attacked me?

Thank you again for your amazing kindness. I think you saved my sanity more than once and I will never forget it. And say goodbye to Derek and tell him how much I appreciated his attention to detail. Jamie

PS Lucinda called. She probably wants you to call back.

He looked at the bright bouquet in the centre of the table and pulled out the little pink card nestled among the stems. "Darling Jamie, we're so sorry about your accident, hope you get better soon. Much love from Prissy and Harriet xxx"

He knew those names, he met them at Tony's place for drinks, and possibly somewhere else as well. Tony or his wife would know how to get in touch with them. Absent-mindedly Leo picked a chocolate out of the big box that sat open beside the flowers and popped it in his mouth. So those women either called here, or they had these delivered. Maybe Jamie invited them for a coffee, to keep her company, because how would they have known she was here?

He checked the dishwasher and found two cups with lipstick marks, so those women came for a visit. But what gave Jamie the idea that people might suspect her of ulterior motives? I invited her, thought Leo, well, I didn't invite her, I more or less abducted her. Surely this weird idea didn't spring unprompted from nowhere. Who said something nasty? Her visitors? But he remembered being amused by those women's nearly total lack of inhibitions that afternoon at Tony's, it was coming back to him now, it was at Tony's place and those two were like a comedy duo, but surely not nasty? Or did they make some joke Jamie took seriously? And that PS about Sinda must mean that she called. Did she start asking questions when Jamie answered his phone? He wondered how that call went, and if Sinda got suspicious the day before, when he said he couldn't come to town for a premiere because he had a friend with her arm in plaster staying. And then Sinda called today, and Jamie answered. Disaster!

He called Jamie, but her phone was offline. He sent a text and an email. His mind was working on two levels at once, and theories and worries competed for attention. In the guest room he looked at the folded sheets, opened the wardrobe door and studied what she had left, and when he turned to leave her room, the laptop caught his eye. It was on a shelf in the wall unit opposite the bed, plugged in and when he lifted the lid, the screen lit up and Jamie was still logged in. Did she leave it on purpose or forget it?

He took it to the living room, sat down at the table and started searching. His email to her had appeared in her Inbox along with an unread message from someone called Louisa. Louisa's message gave him no clues, but he wrote her address on the back of Jamie's letter and ticked the email to make it look unread. At this stage he wasn't prepared to let Jamie see on her phone that someone had read her mail, or she might message people instead. Somehow, he was certain that she was planning to disappear without a trace, to make it impossible for him to track her, everything about her note had a tone of finality. Methodically he opened email after email, checked the messages and listed the addresses of two or three, who appeared to be close friends of Jamie's. Just as he was about to get his own laptop out of his satchel, he had another idea and started checking Jamie's search history. The list of sites told him everything including the time she first thought she must leave and started planning.

Something happened, and it might well have been Sinda's call, he thought, then she started a long series of searches for jobs and accommodation in the wider area. And then she got organized, packed a bag and left. A girl who certainly shouldn't be out there wandering around with concussion and possibly nowhere to go.

The urge to get into the car and start searching was nearly overwhelming, but it was dark outside, he had no idea where she had gone, it would be useless. He needed to make some calls, but for a moment the instinct to do something physical nearly won before common sense made him call Tony first.

'Tony, hi! I need to get in touch with the husband of that couple I met at your place, she's called Harriet and they live in Salcombe, but I can't remember his name or their surname. OK, thanks.'

Tony returned after a talk with his wife, who wanted to find out why Leo wanted to find Harriet's husband and speculated wildly, all of which Leo heard, but finally Tony picked up the phone again.

'They're friends of Clare's, I couldn't even recall his first name. It's Harry, would you believe it? Harriet and Harry Wilson. Clare doesn't have his number, only his wife's – have you got a pen?'

'Hi Harriet,' said Leo a couple of minutes later and tried to sound relaxed. 'Did you visit Jamie this morning? I saw the flowers and the chocolates and I read the card. You did? Great – did she say anything about her plans for the afternoon? She's not here.'

'Really?' Harriet sounded worried. 'But it's dark now and cold, too. Surely, she isn't out walking this late!'

'She's left. I came home a little while ago after a day of meetings in Bath and she's not here. She left a thank-you note and mentioned that people might think she was trying to take advantage of me. Did she say anything like that to you?'

'You're kidding – where on earth did that come from? She didn't say anything about that to us, that's Prissy and me, we went together. We just talked in general about her accident and she said how kind you've been, but nothing about leaving. She did mention that she was going to stay with someone called Louisa – after she leaves your place, I mean. I think she said next weekend, not right now.'

'Could you please ask Prissy to call me if she sees Jamie anywhere or hears anything? You've got my number now, so give her that and say if she hears from Jamie could she please offer her a room for the night or whatever she needs, and to find out where she is - and then call me straight away. And you too, of course.'

'Leo, can I ask you something? I hope you don't mind, but is your flat covered by CCTV?'

'Do you mean inside?'

'Yes.'

'No, it's not.'

'Thank God! You must think I'm mad, but we had the most outrageous conversation this morning and I'd be blushing for days if you could listen to it.'

Leo winced at the thought of what those two might have said, but he felt quite certain now that they hadn't said anything that made Jamie feel she must leave.

What next? Confronting Sinda might clear up some of the questions in his mind, so he checked his phone and noted the time she called and how long the call was.

'Leo, darling!' said Sinda affectionately. 'How lovely to hear from you. How is it down there in the sticks?'

'I see you called today, so you must have spoken to Jamie, my friend who's staying with me. What did you talk about?' He made no attempt to sound friendly.

'Darling, what's the matter? What has she said to you? I just asked where you were, and who she was. I don't think I've ever known your phone to be answered by anyone apart from you or Derek.'

'It was quite a conversation, a bit more than just asking for me. So, what did you say to her? I want the exact words, please!'

'Darling, I'm telling you, I said nothing much, just asked for you and why she was answering your phone, truly, that's all!'

'You told her God knows what and now she's disappeared, concussed and injured and without transport! Now tell me what you said, or I'll never speak to you again.' And even if you do tell me, I might never speak to you again, he thought, while he waited for her to reply. 'Come on, Sinda, tell me!'

Finally, she said, sulky and reluctant, 'I just told her not to take advantage of your good nature. You're a busy man and you don't need distractions. If she says anything else, she's lying.'

'I don't believe you, Sinda! I'm warning you, tell me the truth. Did you call her names? Did you imply she was after me personally, or my money or anything else?'

'Perhaps you should tell *me* something, Leo!' She was furious now, not used to being held to account, hitting back. 'Like, who is Emily? And who is Poppet? And how *dare* you talk about *me* to some stray girl you picked up on the street, and keep secrets from me? Fuck you, Leo!'

He emailed Louisa from his own laptop:

Louisa, you don't know me, but I am a friend of Jamie's. She had an accident, broke her arm and got concussed. She was staying with me, but she went out while I was at work, and she is not back yet. I don't have your phone number. Can you please call me as soon as you get this? Many thanks, Leo Masters

· · ·

He was just about to make something to eat when he remembered that he never told the police about Jamie's attacker, so he called Grindle. 'Sorry to bother you so late, but I've I can't remember the name of the officers who interviewed Jamie in the hospital. She's remembered who attacked her, it was the man she described in the interview. We saw him in a bar in Kingsbridge and he was one of those who blocked the street protest march. Your officers have all the details and they said they'll look for CCTV footage.'

'They found some images on social media,' said Grindle and Leo heard keys tapping. 'I've been following this, seeing I have a personal connection. Hang on while I look it up, yes, here it is. They got a good image of him from the CCTV at the bar, a really good image, full face, and they've got three Facebook posts from the street march with video and photos people posted on the Vista protest group's page. There's a very clear one of him standing face-to-face with Miss Jamieson and you can see she feels disturbed, or maybe threatened.'

'Do you know who he is? He must be local because he kept turning up, followed her on her way to work.'

'We don't know yet, but they're working on it. It won't take long in a small place like that.'

Leo made himself scrambled eggs and toast, poured a glass of wine, and sat down to eat, angry and baffled after the conversation with Sinda. It wasn't until an hour later, when he was drying himself after a shower that he came up with a possible explanation. He stared at his image in the mirror, and while he rubs his hair dry theories and snippets of information that were floating around without connection in his head began to form a credible whole.

Dressed only in boxer shorts, he poured himself another glass of wine and sat in the half dark living room, deep in thought. So, Jamie was ok when Prissy and Harriet left, and then Sinda called and probably called her names and accused her of God knows what. And Jamie got angry, which I really didn't expect - she's usually so in control of herself, she was very cool several times when I overstepped the mark, very cool. Didn't rush in, didn't lose her temper. And to retaliate for whatever Sinda said, she made something up, grabbed a couple of names and pretended I'd told her about them and she must have said I had talked to her about Sinda too. That was smart, very smart, Sinda would have been livid. I don't even know an Emily, and the only Poppet I know is Sophy, I call her poppet sometimes, but when I talk about her, I never call her Poppet. And Sinda's only ever met Sophy once, anyway - I don't want Sinda in my personal life, we just go to events together. But how would Jamie know about Sophy?

And then the penny dropped, and he mentally replayed the phone call with Sophy last night and what he said at his end. Shit! That's it, he thought, of course it is, she heard my side of that conversation, and she heard me say 'goodnight poppet'. I can't believe she let me make love to her if those comments of mine were festering in her mind.

He stayed there looking out over the dark water on the far side of the now quiet road, tried to think of something constructive he could do and failed.

When Louisa called at half past ten Leo was deep in thought and feeling increasingly worried and frustrated; the feeling of powerlessness was not one he was used to.

'Sorry to call so late, I just saw your email. I went to the movies and put my phone on mute. Is Jamie back?'

'No – and I'm very worried about her. I thought she might have called you, or texted. She said to a friend, who visited her this morning, that she might ask if she could stay with you a bit later on.'

'I didn't even know she'd been in an accident! We haven't spoken for a few days. What happened? And why on earth is she staying with you?'

Leo was reluctant to tell her the whole story, to relate personal things about Jamie, but Louisa had known her a lot longer than he had, and he needed her to understand that finding Jamie was urgent. In the back of his mind, fear about Jamie's safety crouched like a brooding beast, scenarios of danger and damage played in an endless loop.

'She fell down the external stairs from her room and was knocked unconscious and broke her arm ...'

'What? She lives in a bungalow style house with an old lady, there aren't any stairs - she sent me photos of the place when she moved in.'

'Listen, she probably hasn't told you yet, she might not want to burden anyone with it, but she lost her job a while ago and had to move to a cheaper place, and she's been living in a room above a factory, with access from an iron stairway on the outside of the building, like a fire escape.'

'Oh God, that's terrible - poor Jamie! And why didn't she tell me? So typical of her, always reluctant to ask for help.' And before Leo could think of an answer she added suspiciously, 'And how come *you* know all this? I thought she was your sworn enemy and now suddenly she's staying at your place?'

'I know it must seem strange, but we were never personal enemies. I mean, she didn't want the Vista development to go ahead, and she was very active in a protest group, but it wasn't against me personally. I think we've developed a great respect for each other and now we're good friends. So, when she had her accident, I offered her a room here until she's recovered.'

Only when the call had ended did he realise that possibly none of Jamie's friends have her new phone number. He texted Louisa and Harriet to tell them the number, failed to think of anyone else who might need to know and finally went to bed.

Chapter 31

It was dawn when Jamie woke up, cold and stiff. She crawled out from under the workbench and indecisively wondered how to start her day. Her sleep had been disturbed by a terrifying nightmare that woke her up in a state of panic and took a long time to recover from, and then several episodes of waking, thinking she heard something and sleeping lightly in between. A quick glance through the window showed no sign of life at the kitchen window and nobody in the garden. She unplugged the phone, stuffed the charger back into the bag, and turned the phone on.

A missed call from Leo and a voice message:

Jamie, it's Leo. Please call me and tell me where you are. I'm really worried now. I'm sorry about last night – I took advantage and it won't happen again, you owe me nothing. Please get in touch as soon as you hear this.

. . .

A text message from Leo:

Listen to your voice mail, I need to know you're OK. Leo

A second text message from Leo:

Please Jamie, this is driving me mad. Call me or at least tell me you're safe. You left your laptop behind. Leo

An email from Leo:

Jamie — please come back or at least reply. I am very worried, and I need to know if you are safe somewhere or if I should call the police. I made a mistake and I don't want you to think you have to have sex with me to pay me back for anything. I made love to you because I have been attracted to you from when I saw you at the lawyers and I was already attracted to your calmly feisty persona Sandy too, though I didn't understand why at the time. Please get in touch. Yours, Leo

She read and re-read the messages. He sounded genuine, as if he was really worried that she'd think he took sex for granted, like something due to him — it was so confusing. If she hadn't heard that phone conversation, she would take all this at face value, but what was the truth? What she felt for him now was far too serious to risk getting the basic understanding wrong, or to treat it as a casual affair. To be close to him again and then find out he really didn't understand the sort of person she was would be heart-breaking. Or to have it turn into something as damaging as her relationship with Douglas, which might crumble her self-confidence forever. She didn't think she had it in her to recover from that kind of trauma a second time, so it was better to not have any further contact, however painful that would be; loss and grief was better than destruction. She would let him know she was safe, but nothing else.

Chapter 32

At half past five Leo lay on his back staring at the ceiling and considered what he knew and what he could make a guess at, and one thing was clear, he must talk to Louisa again as soon as possible. It was vital to make her understand what he thought the problem was, but waiting was torture. It was too early to call, reading was beyond him and after a while he couldn't lie still any longer, so he got out of bed and dressed. Finally at quarter to seven, when the sun would appear over the horizon in ten or fifteen minutes, he picked up his phone.

'Sorry to call you so early, Louisa, but I want to fill you in and ask for your help. I haven't heard from Jamie yet, have you? No? Well, I want to tell you a story that will probably take ... say ten minutes, and then I'll explain what it is you can help me with.'

'OK, but I've got to be ready to leave for work at quarter past eight at the latest and I have to shower and wash my hair.'

Quickly he told her everything in verbal bullet points, from the first time he saw Sandy the protester and the first time he saw Jamie, not realising it was the same person. He told her all the relevant details of how they came to trust each other and how he more or less abducted her from the hospital. When he said that Jamie's so-called accident was really an attack, Louisa interrupted. 'Is this true? That man either threw her or dropped her from that height onto a paved lane and she survived? It sounds unbelievable – like she could have died.'

'I think she was very lucky the way she fell. The doctor at the emergency department said that sometimes people survive horrendous falls without serious damage because they kind of twist and hit the ground at an angle somehow, nearly roll with the momentum. I imagine her arm, the one that broke, acted as a kind of shock absorber. No fractured ribs or shoulders.'

'Right, I can kind of picture that – sorry, go on and tell me more.'

He explained why the police got involved and what they were doing, and then he reached the hard part.

'I have to find her, Louisa! I can't bear to think she's without comfort or money and that she might have those terrible nightmares and nobody around to get her through them. I don't know if she feels anything for me, but she thinks that I believe she's mercenary and that I suspect her of seeing me as an opportunity, for money, marriage or status, and I don't know what. And I think that's why she left. She couldn't bear that I should think that, or that anyone should think that.'

Explaining how he came to this conclusion stretched his patience to the limit. He knew it, but it was hard to explain the process he went through to someone else, so it made coherent sense. He tried to boil down and link all the ideas and guesses he made, he told her about Sinda's call and the note Jamie left.

'But I think the crucial thing that happened was that she probably heard the end of a phone conversation about Pride and Prejudice I had the night before last.'

'What? Why is that a problem? And excuse me for being personal, Leo, but you've never seemed to me the kind of man who'd read Jane Austen. Not that I've met you, but I read about you now and then.'

'Well, I *am* reading it, someone told me I should, and we've been discussing it on the phone a couple of times a week. You know, like comparing notes and discussing the character's motivation for doing and saying what they do. And by the way, it's brilliant social satire, isn't it? And I know exactly what Jamie heard and misunderstood the night before last when she woke up from her nap and I was on the phone in the living room with the door half open. We were discussing why Charlotte Lucas agreed to marry Mr Collins, what her strongest motivation was, seeing it certainly wasn't love or lust. The person I was talking to thought it was because Charlotte knew it might be her only chance to have children of her own or she wanted to avoid the status of spinster whatever the price. And I said I thought – well, you can imagine.'

There was no need to explain further, Louisa laughed briefly. 'Oh my God – don't tell me Jamie heard you expound of Charlotte's reasons, like position in society, security, the consequence of being a married woman and all that. Oh, you poor idiot man, you're in deep trouble now!'

'I know,' he said meekly. 'Total stuff-up, it took me hours of thinking and trying to put two and two together before I figured it out. So, here's how you can help, provided you want to help me?'

'I would dig ditches in the rain, if it would help you, now that I've heard the story! I'm not sure that you deserve Jamie, she's a very special person, but I'll do my best. What do you want me to do?'

'It's more what I want you not to do. I've not told you yet, but Jamie left her laptop behind, probably her bag was getting too heavy or too full and she has her phone, so the laptop isn't strictly necessary. But she forgot to log off, she just put it on the shelf in her room, closed the lid and plugged it in to charge – she has memory lapses from the concussion. And when I opened it, there it was, still running in sleep-mode, everything available, including her Google search history. I opened her emails and that's how I got your address.'

'You know what? I never even thought of that when you sent that message. But never mind, I think I can see where this is going. You're hoping to find out where she is, and it's important that I don't tell her we've been talking.'

'Exactly! If you really want to help, you might even send her an email, perhaps you could ask how life in Kingsbridge is going or something like it, but don't for God's sake let on that we've been talking. I *could* look at her reply to your email, but it seems intrusive in case she tells you very personal things, so I thought I'd turn off her laptop, and then you can call me or email me and tell me where she is. If you think I should know.'

'I'll text you and tell you what I find out, but on one condition,' said Louisa firmly. 'So tell me honestly, Leo – I've got to know if this is driven by attraction and lust, or if it's something more enduring. Do you love her?'

'Yes,' was all he said, and Louisa laughed again. 'Good man! I'll send her an email later today. Sorry, but I've got to start getting ready for work in a hell of a hurry now.'

'Where do you work? God! This is all so back to front - I've just realised I know nothing about you.'

'I teach senior French and English and I wrote my master's thesis on how Jane Austen's uses her characters to illustrate the status of women in Georgian and Regency England. May I suggest that you pick up your copy of Pride and Prejudice and read the very first sentence in the book again?'

'I will – and thank you! I am very grateful.'

He turned on his Kindle and went back to the first chapter: "It is universally acknowledged that a single man in possession of a good fortune must be in want of a wife."

Chapter 33

Sitting in the early bus waiting to depart, Jamie watched what might be her last glimpse of Kingsbridge for a long time. With all that had happened here, the mixture of joy and fun and heartache, the town would always be part of her personal history, but she can't imagine returning any time soon. Possibly for a visit when Gemma and William come back, she thought and blinked through tears at the glare of the morning sun suddenly cresting the buildings and shining through the window beside her.

'Is this seat taken?' asked a woman with two children, and Jamie looked up, puzzled by the question. The woman smiled. 'My kids always sit beside each other on the bus, so I have to find a seat immediately behind, they like it better than me sitting across the aisle, and there are two empty seats in front of you.'

'This seat is free,' said Jamie and watched as the mother lifted the two small children up on the seats in front of her and handed them each a plastic box from her large shopping bag.

'Snacks and diversions,' she said briskly and sat down beside Jamie. 'We do this once a week, it's routine now.'

'How old are they?'

'The girl is nearly five and the boy is three. She's extremely bossy and acts as if she's his mother. He rebels occasionally, but generally he does what he's told. Works a treat on the bus, we go every week to see my grandmother who lives in Torquay.' She half-rose and looked over the backs of the seats in front of them, then sat down again. 'I'm the only relative living close enough to visit her and she loves seeing the kids. We always go on this bus, so we arrive in time for morning tea - she's a great scone maker, my grandma.' She pulled a magazine from her bag and started reading.

I never thought of it before, thought Jamie, but I've never had anything to do with very small children, no siblings, no cousins, never babysat for anyone and the only friends, who have children are Di and Brodie and theirs is only a baby I haven't seen for six months.

A couple of times the children's mother got up and stood in the aisle talking to them and Jamie listened, intrigued.

'You talk to them as if they're adults,' she said. 'I don't know the first thing about children, but I sort of expected you to ... I don't know quite what. Talk to them differently?'

'Perhaps we'd better introduce ourselves? I'm Carla,

those two are Ara and Angus. And yes, I've always talked to them as if they're adults – I think it's because I always talk to my cat as if he's an adult, and I just continued with the kids.'

They talked intermittently during the forty-five minute trip and gradually Jamie began to feel as if her life were normal, though in a different way from before. After the stress of the last few days, when she felt like a refugee in a foreign country where other people made decisions and moved her around, she was now in control of her life again.

'What happened to your arm?' asked Carla, and to her surprise Jamie found herself telling the story, not normally something she would go into detail about with a casual acquaintance; so personal and traumatic.

'What an awful experience – you poor thing! And the only thing you broke was your arm, falling from a height like that? You were incredibly lucky.'

'And bruises and concussion, and in the last day or so I've realised one of my hips is very sore, so maybe it's a good thing I can't ride my bike.'

'And why are you going to Torquay? Do you live there?'

'No, but I'm moving there. The rest of my things will be delivered in a few days – I just took what I need.' She noticed Carla's eyes roving over her face and wondered what she had said to warrant that searching look. 'I've applied for some jobs there and I've got my accommodation sorted out, so I thought I might as well be on the spot in case I get an interview. And my car was stolen and not replaced yet, so it's been a bit of a mission making the move.'

'You seem to have a lot of bad luck lately! Did you apply for the job at Hawkstone's, the bookshop?'

'I don't think I even saw it. Is there a job going there?'

'There was last week when we walked past, they had a sign in the window. Mind you, the old guy who owns the place might not even know how to put a job vacancy ad on the Internet, that sign might be the full extent of his advertising. He's like something from a bygone age.'

'I'd like to work in a bookshop,' said Jamie. 'I really would! I love reading and you'd get to talk with a lot of interesting people about which books to buy - lovely.'

Carla laughed. 'You'd better head straight there from the bus and check if the job is still going. You can walk with us, if you like, we go right past on the way to grandma.'

As they set out from the bus stop, Ara decided that Jamie was her friend and insisted on walking right beside her, so they were obliged to drop behind Carla and the stroller, when they met people.

'Sorry,' she said when they were walking abreast again after a diversion. 'What did you just say about Facebook?'

'I asked if you belong to the Protect Wellby protest group – they have a page on Facebook.'

Jamie was baffled by the out-of-the-blue questions, but it must mean something, maybe she had missed something when she and Ara fell behind. 'Yes, I'm a member of the group,' she replied cautiously.

'I knew it! I thought I must have seen you somewhere

before – it's that video clip on Facebook, from the street march. You were right at the front, but you had a cap on then, so today your hair confused me.'

Jamie felt anxious, though she couldn't think why she should be. This woman was no threat to her; it must be the memory of when she stood face-to-face with her attacker for the first time that still made her so uncomfortable. Should she tell Carla? And then she realised that if she did, there was a slight possibility that she might know who he was.

'Does the video show how that gang of men came straight at us, with the long banner in front of them?'

'Oh, yes, the person who filmed it must have been standing nearly exactly where you met. And you turned your head to the side, you looked disgusted, and I thought maybe the man in front of you had said something nasty – I noticed him grinning.'

'He had, and he's the one who attacked me, just a few days after the march.'

'Oh my God – did the cops get him?'

'Not that I know of, but it's one of the reasons I'm moving so quickly without all my things. I can't bear the thought of him catching sight of me again, or what he might do.'

Ten minutes later Carla pointed across the street. "There it is, and I can see the notice still on the window from here.'

'Thank you! I'll go across and ask.'

Carla pulled Ara towards her. 'Good luck! I'll pop in and check if you got hired when I come over next week.'

'Assistant wanted for Tue, Wed, Thu, Fri and occasional Sat mornings. Enquire within.' The notice was handwritten with what looked like ink. Fountain pen! thought Jamie. I don't think I've ever seen anyone write with a fountain pen, apart from perhaps some president on TV signing important papers. But Heather had one, I remember being allowed to use it when I was seven and trying to learn calligraphy – how quaint.

A bell tinkled when she pushed the door open and then she was in another world, one that felt old and borderline magical; a big high-ceilinged room lit by lights on long cords with white glass shades. Bookshelves with elaborate finials on the top corners lined the walls and small four-sided shelf units were scattered in the open space. Each of the freestanding shelves had a white card mounted on a finial with a topic written in cursive script with curlicues on the capitals. She stopped just inside the door, looked around and read the signs: geography, politics, health, botany, philosophy, vampires. Vampires? She was so absorbed in taking it all in that she failed to notice the man who had silently appeared beside her.

'Good morning! Can I help you?' He was a short man in his seventies, with crinkly grey hair and round, gold-rimmed spectacles.

'I saw your sign in the window and I'd like to apply for the job, if it hasn't been taken already.'

'Not yet, come with me.' There was no introduction, no shaking of hands, just a few words and then he guided her to one side and stopped in front of the wall shelves. 'Do you know who Thackeray was?'

'Yes, he wrote *Vanity Fair* – in the nineteenth century.'

'Good, and have you heard of Audrey Niffenegger?'

'She wrote *The Time Traveller's Wife*, quite a few years ago. And then another novel about a pair of twins, which wasn't half as good.'

'Geraldine Brooks?'

'No, sorry.'

He seemed impressed that she had heard of *Silent Spring*, though she couldn't remember the name of the author.

'What do you know about Stephen Hawking?'

She gave him a brief but comprehensive two-minute lecture on Stephen Hawking and dark matter, and he smiled. 'Well, I did ask far that, didn't I? You're very well informed.'

It's test of general book knowledge, thought Jamie. He doesn't want anyone working here who isn't familiar, at least by name, with well-known writers, whatever the genre. They continued slowly around the shop and by the time he stopped asking questions, they had covered just about every kind of fiction and some specialist topics. Her head was aching furiously, but she steeled herself to concentrate, because she really wanted to work here. It was clear that the places where he stopped to ask questions, bore no relation to the authors or topic that he was asking her about. She tried to answer his questions and study the shelves at the same time, suspecting there was a logic behind this unconventional way of conducting a job interview. When they finally reached the counter, on the opposite side from where they had started, he stuck his hand out. 'Bernard,' he said. 'My name's Bernard, what's yours?'

'Jamie, well, my real name is Alexandra Jamieson, but I'm always called Jamie.'

'When can you start?'

She nearly laughed out loud. This would make a lovely setting for a TV comedy, a quaint bookshop with an eccentric owner where she felt anything could happen.

'I can start tomorrow if you want. I'm moving here from Kingsbridge, but I haven't even been to see the room I enquired about, because someone on the bus told me you had a sign in the window, so I came here first.'

'Good, come in at ten tomorrow morning. We close at half past five, apart from Saturday when we close at two, and we're closed on Sundays and Mondays. I have another assistant, Robbie, but he's gone to do some errands for me. He'll be back soon, so if you wait you can meet him. Did you notice anything in particular when we walked around the shelves?'

'Only that the authors are arranged alphabetically, in reverse order - from right to left instead of the usual way.'

'Very good! You're observant and you can think while you talk – excellent!' He looked at her bag still sitting just inside the door. 'Where are you going to stay?'

She told him and he shook his head. 'You'd better take a taxi, that's way up a very steep street. You've got that bag, and with your arm in plaster you can't even change hands.'

'I haven't got all my clothes yet, my luggage is coming later. Is it all right if I wear jeans and a nice top to work?'

He's so old fashioned, she thought, and so eccentric, he might expect me to wear a skirt. But Bernard, whose surname she had yet to discover, surprised her.

'Jeans are fine,' he said with a grin, amused that she had been taken in. 'I wear jeans myself in my spare time, but I've become known for always wearing a tweed jacket and a bow tie, so that's what I do. People even take selfies of themselves with me and post them on social media, very funny! And very good for business, we're on Trip Advisor, too.' She could see how much he had enjoyed surprising her. 'I'm not a relic from a bygone age, I do have a computer and a smartphone. I just like the shop to look like it always did, and as I said, my appearance is expected now, people come visiting from all over to buy books here and talk to me. I've become a so called "personality". And then they go out with their purchases and say, "isn't he such a character?" Welcome to Hawkstone's, Jamie!'

The room at Mr Whittleston's house was not quite as small as he had led her to believe. It was perfectly square with a tall, narrow window in the white-washed stone wall and faded pink and green curtains.

'This is fine,' said Jamie, when he opened the door and stood back, looking slightly worried. 'Plenty big enough for one person. Is there a bathroom I can use?'

'I had another bathroom put in upstairs when I

decided to let rooms – after my wife died. I converted the sewing room, as my wife used to call it. So, there's one bathroom up there that I use, and then the new one that the woman who rents the second bedroom upstairs uses. I'm sure you can share it. There's a toilet just off the downstairs hall too.'

'Will I be able to cook in your kitchen?'

'Sara, the other renter, she cooks for herself and for me, we made a deal. I can't cook and she likes cooking, so I charge her less rent and she cooks. I'm sure you two can fit in with each other.'

Look at that smile, thought Jamie. He's so pleased with his domestic arrangement. If Sara isn't keen on sharing the kitchen with me, I'll just eat like I did in the last place, or eat out. At least I'll have an income again, even if I forgot to ask Bernard what he's going to pay me. I can buy an electric kettle and make breakfast in my room.

He left her and she sat down on the single bed, looked around the little room and considered her options. The room was good enough, and she liked looking out over the garden. The empty bookshelf would be convenient for her clothes as there was no chest of drawers, and she would move the little table next to the bed and put the chair in the corner. All she needed was a little lamp for beside the bed, and if Mr Whittlestone didn't have one she would buy a cheap one, but there was nowhere to put her boxes, so somehow, she must solve that problem before she needed warmer clothes for winter, though she had no idea how she could do this.

She left to house half an hour later with Mr Whittleston's spare key and an admonition to make sure she always checked that the front door was locked when she went out. The street ran down towards the town centre like a stream on a hillside, tracing a winding course, where now and then on a corner she caught a glimpse of the harbour and the sea, and felt her spirit lift.

The café she picked at random has a surprising range of food and the 'all day breakfast' of bacon and eggs with toast made a perfect main meal for the day. Jotting down a couple of things on a paper napkin turned into a list that grew while she ate. She studied the scrawl and hoped she would be able to decipher it later; the cast made holding a pen clumsy, and the more she wrote the worse her handwriting became. The letter she had written to Leo had become an embarrassing scrawl by the time she reached the end, but trying to connect to his printers hadn't been an option; that thank-you letter had to be written by hand.

She re-read her list: Check emails, Skype Gemma, Skype Louisa, what to do about the boxes, buy 2 nice shirts and indoor shoes, check car insurance, contact the storage unit, cancel rent on the ghastly garret. The relief of having a job so soon was immeasurable, and now she dared spend some of her savings. She ordered another cup of coffee and got her phone out.

Chapter 34

Leo had read Jamie's long message so many times he knew it by heart:

I'm sorry you were worried. I don't want you to feel that way after being so kind. I'm perfectly safe. I spent the night in Kingsbridge, but I had to turn my phone off and didn't see your messages. I'm now in another town, where I have booked a low-priced but safe room and I've found a job. I'll repay you bit by bit. Please don't think you took advantage, I said yes, the attraction is mutual. I'll retrieve the laptop later, the phone will do for now. Thank you for everything you did for me, I never thought a man like you could possibly exist, you made me feel so safe and looked after. Jamie'

He tried to tease out what she felt, the truth behind the wording that was like a barrier she had erected to hide her real feelings. Behind those calm and minimal statements must lie a welter of feelings: hurt, worry, loneliness and possibly anger. She was clearly determined to distance herself, but the news that she was not in Kingsbridge was a relief. Having moved away she should be safe. His immediate instinct, when he first discovered she had left, had been to drive to Kingsbridge and check the buses, ask questions, try to work out where she had gone, but he was calmer now. A voice of warning in the back of his mind was telling him to step back. *I can't do that, she has the right to leave and if she wants to keep me from knowing where she is, I have to abide by that. I'll have to watch myself or I'll turn into a stalker.* He sighed, put the phone down and went to get ready for work.

That night, when he was halfway through cooking dinner with a glass of wine beside him, Louisa called. He turned off the stove, picked up his glass and sat down at the table. 'Any news?'

'She called about an hour ago. I sent her an email in my morning break — I nearly made a fatal error and texted her, and how would I have explained how I knew her new number? So, she called and we talked for ages. Some of what she told me is very personal and I don't feel I can share all the details without her permission, but there are a few things I can tell you.'

'Is she ok? And safe?' He told her about Jamie's text message, then he read it out and Louisa laughed. 'That's classic Jamie — carefully thought out and worded, nothing given away by accident, no inferences to be drawn. That girl's going to be a fantastic barrister if she completes her degree, isn't she?'

'Was she studying law? I didn't know.'

'She only had one year left and she was an outstanding student, so the result was guaranteed. She wanted to do court work – she was fascinated by the debate-like aspect of putting arguments across. But then her mother got more and more muddled, and she felt she had to take a break from her studies and go and live in Kingsbridge to support her for a while, and it became two years. And that's how we got to where we are today, in a complete mess.'

'Did you find out if her accommodation is safe? It really worries me that she might be living in a dreadful room in some unsafe place to save money until she gets a job.'

'She seems to be safe enough. I don't think she's in any danger from the man who attacked her, and there's no reason to think where she's living isn't perfectly fine. It's a house that belongs to an old man and he's got another woman renting a room as well, someone a bit older who's been there for some time. And she's got a job already in a lovely bookshop owned by some crazy original who looks like someone out of a 1940's comedy. Apparently, the shop is quite famous, and people come to visit after reading about it on Trip Advisor. She was very lucky, the job wasn't on the internet, but she saw the sign in the window and got the job on the spot.' She paused and Leo could nearly feel her hesitating. 'And you were totally right about her reasons for leaving. She did overhear that phone conversation and she took for granted you were talking about her. And of course, she still thinks that - I couldn't tell her otherwise.'

'Fuck!' he said quietly, as if to himself, and then more loudly, 'Anything else you can share?'

'Yes, and I'm doing this with some hesitation, Leo, and only because I love Jamie and I think you're the man she wants - and you're probably also the man she needs. She didn't say so, but it's pretty obvious. You were totally on the way to winning her complete devotion, or you already have it. I know how to read between the lines with Jamie, the subtext she doesn't write or say, but it's there. But she has this thing about relationships based on past experience, a very bad experience.'

'Do you think it would be better not to tell me?' He wasn't sure now that he wanted to know very personal things about Jamie's life. What if we meet again, he thought, what about when she contacts me about those boxes? And I know things, personal things, and she's not aware that I know. Is that going to create another problem between us?

But when he voiced this fear to Louisa, she sounded very certain. 'No, you need to know this, so you understand what's going on in her head. When I said I was hesitating it's because she doesn't tell people herself, and I've always kept her past to myself. So, if I tell you, it's got to be on the condition of discretion from your side, but you need to understand why she fled from you. Because that's what she did, she fled out of fear that she would once again find herself in a situation like the one with Douglas. That she would be unable to resist a relationship with you because she adores you. As I said earlier, she didn't say that, but it's what I feel – she's terrified that the relationship would turn toxic and it would break her, this time it really would. Nobody survives two destructive relationships. That was the risk she fled from.'

'OK, explain it to me, please.'

'She got together with Douglas before I knew her, she was about seventeen at the time and after two years he had crushed her spirit. I mean crushed, destroyed. I became a sort of friend at one remove, when she and Douglas were halfway through the relationship, but I didn't often see them together. He was very controlling, and he didn't like me or any of her woman friends, actually. I knew him for what he was after the first evening I spent with them in company. I've rarely seen such total domination and such blatant passive aggression. When I got to know her, she was just about to turn down the university scholarship she had won, and her self-esteem was at rock bottom. He was older, about eight or ten years older and he dominated her.' Louisa hesitated for a moment. 'He's a public person now, a media personality, quite well-known and I don't want any of this repeated, Leo.'

'I won't, anything we talk about stays between us.'

'OK then, these are some stray phrases she used today, when she told me her reasons for leaving you. I jotted down some of the key things on my pad while we spoke, so this is not verbatim, but it's close enough. She said things like, I'm afraid of getting caught up in something demoralizing again. I'll never again risk being always at a disadvantage, constantly feeling under scrutiny, found wanting, having to justify, have sarcasm heaped on me every day. It saps your mental strength and your self-belief. It turns you into a husk. You end up with no soul to call your own. You always try to please, to prove something, to earn the other person's love. Never again.'

'Christ! That Douglas guy must have been something else. Was he a control freak or did he think he was better than Jamie, or what was it?'

'I think he knew from the start that she loved him a lot more than he loved her, if he ever really loved her at all, maybe he just wanted her around because she's so gorgeous, like a trophy. He controlled her by making her feel inadequate. She told me once that she begged him to give her a second chance, when they broke up once very early on. She pleaded with him to take her back and promised that she would never disappoint him again and change and be better - image! It was like giving him permission to turn into a ruthless despot, wasn't it?'

'It's sounds like a bloody awful thing to happen a teenager, or anyone for that matter,' said Leo, devastated on Jamie's behalf. 'But it's hard to reconcile this with what I've seen of her. I mean, she's so together and in control of herself - and she can't be talked down, not even by a redneck shouting from the back of a hall. If that was what that Douglas character did to her, she's made a stunning recovery. How long ago did this happen?'

'She left him when she was nineteen, she's twenty-four now I think, no she's twenty-five. I'd known her for about a year at the time, and she came and stayed in my spare room until the end of her first year at university, which was perfect, because I could support her and coach her and help her through the worst. I'm fourteen years older than Jamie and I knew a bit more about life and men than she did. Her mother was living in Taunton, where Jamie grew up, and she wasn't much help, she simply didn't understand the workings of that kind of abusive relationship. But even so, I've never understood how she could let a girl that age go off with a man ten years her senior to live in another city. Negligent or reckless I call it. And you say you can't reconcile it with the Jamie you've seen in action – well, that Jamie is probably the original Jamie inside an armour of her own making, to keep herself safe. She's not had a relationship on any level since Douglas. Maybe casual sex, but I doubt she's even had that. She is scarred, Leo!'

Leo thought of the expression on her face when she told him about the man facing her at the street march, how the up-close, face to face aggression had such a terrible effect on her. The way she described him calling her 'darling' and using the word as a weapon. Because she had endured this before, she was re-living the past. And the way she had reacted to the same man in the bar, even when he was just looking at her. He had felt how strong her urge to get up and flee was. Damaged, he thinks, unable to control fear in the face of aggressive bullying, but capable of keeping her cool and finish what she wants to say in a hall with men yelling at her from the back - complex and interesting.

Louisa had paused and he thought she had finished, but she continued and now she sounded as if she was close to tears. 'You should have seen her then, Leo. A frail looking girl, very young-looking for her age, with that incredible white skin and a mane of thick red hair. She looked other-worldly, like an illustration in an old-fashioned story book. People turned around for a second look when they met her in the street. And she was totally unaware, she had no idea how unusual and appealing she was and still is.'

'She's exactly like that, Louisa, I've never known anyone like her. That fragile appearance and the determination, and the focus. She could rule the world without raising her voice. What you've told me makes me want to cry for her.'

'I think I was right about you, Leo. You'll do!' He heard the relief in her voice, she was not regretting telling him.

Grindle's text message arrived nearly the same moment that he ended the call with Louisa.

Miss Jamieson's attacker identified. Two previous investigations for violence against women, one prison sentence for serious assault and rape eight years ago, out of prison one year ago. Seems to have turned up in Kingsbridge in the last couple of months, originally from Liverpool. CCTV from tractor business shows his car, he walked into the lane at 5.49. Arrest warrant issued and alerts for his car circulated. Two previous victims were redheads.

Just before he turned his bedside light off, there was another long text from Jamie:

I have a solution for the boxes. I have a job and a bit more money. I'll organize someone to pick up the boxes and take them to a storage unit where I have a piece of furniture stored. I'll ask that person to bring a bolt cutter and cut the padlock off the door and attach a new one. At your end it would mean telling my hired helper when they can pick the boxes up without inconveniencing you. I think I left the laptop charging. I've only just realised. Could put it in one of the boxes, please? Thanks, Jamie

After thinking of the pros and cons he replied:

Dear Jamie, please let Derek do this for you. He was devastated to hear that you had left and that I don't know where you are. In his opinion I have failed you, I can tell what he's thinking. He'd love to do something practical to help you and I promise not to interfere in the process in any way. You've arrange it directly with him. The police have identified your attacker and are looking for him now. I have given Plymouth police your new phone number. I miss you. Leo. PS I called Sinda.

. . .

After dinner Leo tried in vain to get some work done, anything to take his mind off what was becoming an obsession. His worries seemed to pile up and interlock like a jigsaw puzzle and once he started thinking of one, the others intruded and created tangle: worrying about Jamie despite all Louisa's reassurances about her safety, wondering if Jamie was missing him, telling himself he mustn't try to identify that bookshop, worrying that he was turning into a stalker. What would Jamie think about the PS he had added as a bait at the end of the message? Maybe, just maybe, she'd ask what happened when he talked to Sinda, and then they could have at least one more exchange of messages. He was sure she wouldn't call him or answer if he called her, but maybe they could have a message conversation. Any opportunity for him to insert some kind of explanation in a natural way about that phone call. I wish I could understand why I am so reluctant to simply send her a text message and explain it, he thought, but I can't, damn it - I just can't.

Chapter 35

Jamie was sitting on her bed, which was far more comfortable than the little armchair, which had a broken spring in a very inconvenient spot; she was contemplating her surprisingly satisfactory day. The faded chintz curtains were pulled across the window and the little lamp Mr Whittleston had lent her cast a circle of light over the round table beside the bed. She thought back to waking up at dawn, lying under the workbench in Gemma's shed, wondering if she had no options left, if her life was going to be an endless struggle. Only fifteen hours ago, but it seemed like something she experienced a week ago. Looking back, she understood that spending the night in Gemma's shed had been an over-reaction, and worrying about money didn't quite explain why she had done it; there was more to it than that.

She reasoned through it in her mind, that probably the concussion was still making her process things differently from what she would normally, that she seemed to experience very strong fears and reactions to things around her. And that she could only see that she had over-reacted when she looked back, as if she only saw thing in proportion after she had reacted. But such good things had happened today that it made up for yesterday to some degree. Today had diluted the anxiety she was feeling, the fear that she would bump into the man who attacked her or not find a job. And shopping for two nice shirts to wear to work with her jeans was a reassuringly normal thing to do, and a bargain. And she loved the bookshop, that treasure trove run by a benevolent goblin; she couldn't wait to start working there.

The added bonus of already feeling at home in this room, something she never did in the room above the factory, the neatness of her clothes folded on the shelves and the new shirts hanging on the hooks behind the door. She looked down at her legs in the silky pink and grey striped pyjamas that Leo had bought for her. There was a lump in her throat, and she held back tears with an effort of will.

I love him, she thought, and ran her hand over the pyjama leg, and I miss him so much. Just my luck to fall for someone who regards me as a scheming go-getter. If he hadn't been so lovely and kind, so caring, I might have managed to pretend I wasn't falling in love with him. I 've struggled against the attraction I felt for him ever since I first set eyes on him. Trying to kid myself into thinking it was just some form of lust was ridiculous, I knew all along it was something quite different, like I could sense the good qualities in him. As soon as I got to know him properly, I knew I was in serious trouble. I did try to fight it off, but he got under my skin so fast and now he's fixed there, I can't banish him from my thoughts. I nearly wish I hadn't heard that phone conversation, but then sooner or later it would have become apparent that he was watching for the moves I would make to snare him, and that would have been so humiliating and painful. It was such a relief to talk to Louisa today, she always listens and really gets what you mean, and I think she understood why I had to leave. I'll talk to her again soon. I must do something about those boxes, I think the plan I thought up is OK. The only negative today was meeting Sara, who obviously resents me being here. Sharing a bathroom with her will be a balancing act, so I think maybe I'll stay right out of the kitchen, until I'm sure she and Mr Whittleston have had their meal each night and I'll keep it simple, single-serve frozen meals or tins or something - it's all food and I can't be fussy. Or I could buy another little microwave oven.

She composed her carefully worded message about the boxes and let the phone rest on the bed beside her for several minutes before she re-read the text and pressed Send. Within minutes she had Leo's reply, and his PS threw her into a state of deep uncertainty. What could it possibly mean? Had he talked to Sinda and been told lies, or was he simply saying that he followed her advice and called her? Why did she herself put a PS about Sinda at the end of the note she left for him? A PS kind of highlighted whatever you said, more so than if it was just a sentence in the middle of the text. It wasn't just an afterthought, it could be a way of signalling something, mentioning the important bit last so it stayed in the mind of the person who read it. Did she want him to take note, to know that Sinda represented something important? She didn't know why she had done it, maybe her subconscious had been trying to make sure he would pay attention, realise that Sinda was linked to her leaving and that she was a nasty woman.

The words 'I miss you' in Leo's message brought his physical presence into sharp focus in her mind, black haired, stern faced and kind-hearted. The sensation of his stubbly cheek rasping against hers, his arm and leg anchoring her terrified body and making her feel safe, his voice calm and certain. She remembered hearing his heartbeat, strong and steady and how that made her feel, and now she did cry, silently and without wiping the tears from her cheeks. She felt with a certainty that devastated her, that she would never find anyone like him again, never feel that sensation of being totally safe. I thought that mentally we were equals, she thought sadly, despite the difference in age and wealth and nearly everything else. I thought he saw me differently, realised that I'm genuine and have integrity. I'll reply to his text about Derek tomorrow when I feel calmer.

. . .

When the phone pinged that a text had arrived, her hand darted out to pick up the phone and her heart beat faster. Was it another message from Leo? It was from the same unknown number as a call that afternoon that she hadn't taken and not listened to the voice message from either. But it was from Harriet, and Jamie felt confused and once again a bit worried. How did Harriet know her new phone number, did she give it to her and then forgot? But the message made it clear:

Darling Jamie, I just have to text you, Leo gave me your number, I hope you don't mind. He got hold of me and told me you had left, he was beside himself the poor man, and I couldn't tell him anything useful. But I'm so worried about you, I can't understand why you did this, are you sure your concussion isn't doing things to your mind? Please tell me you're OK and if you need ANYTHING just call me! I'll pick you up from wherever you are and take you home to our place and you can stay with us for as long as you like! Big hug! Harriet xxx

It was getting late now, and Jamie was sleepy, but Harriet's message left her feeling that she must work out how this happened, how had Leo known to contact Harriet. In her mind she went through the events of yesterday morning: Harriet and Prissy arriving with chocolates and flowers, having coffee, the call from Sinda, leaving Leo's apartment – somewhere in the middle of this there was a clue. It was only when she tiptoed out to the toilet in the dark hall that it came to her, and she understood how it hung together. There was a little pink card with the flowers, and Harriet and Prissy told her they had met Leo at someone's house for drinks. Of course, he simply tracked down Harriet's number and called her, then he gave her the new phone number, but what else did he do or say? Did he ask Harriet to find out where she was? And would she then tell him if she knew? The thought of a face-to-face meeting with Leo was more than she could bear to think of just now. Would she have the strength of mind to tell him to go away, if he were right there in front of her?

She replied with a soothing message to Harriet, careful not to apportion blame or tell her any details, just that it wasn't working out staying at Leo's, and that she was fine, she was safe and had a job. She ended by asking Harriet to let Prissy know and said, 'you two lovely, kind women, please give each other a hug from me, I miss you already!'

Chapter 36

In his silent Salcombe apartment Leo glanced at his buzzing phone before he picked it up, hoping against hope that it would be Jamie, but it wasn't, of course.

'How are you, poppet?' he said and made an effort to sound cheerful. 'How was your week?' His conversations with Sophy were usually a high point when he was away from home, but it was hard to sound positive when he was feeling so low.

'Oh, good. My new history teacher is so cool, and the work she sets for us is so interesting, and it's quite hard - but she said we are getting ready for university now, so we have to be able to deal with it. But I think I already regret dropping economics. Maybe I should have kept it for this final year, such a useful subject and it made me seem so intelligent, because I was good at it, and people thought I was really smart.'

'You are really smart, full stop, so that's nothing to worry about. Do you want me to ask if you can change?'

Sophy laughed. 'God, no – please don't, I'm a big girl now, Leo! I'll ask them myself if I really want to change, but I don't think I will. Do you want to hear about Margot?'

'What has she done now? Not another boy disaster?'

'Oh no, *much* worse, she crashed her dad's BMW last weekend, the big model, not her mum's little one – nearly totalled it. She wasn't supposed to drive it at all, but she did. And it was pretty new, too, so her parents are absolutely furious, and they don't even *know* yet that she was racing someone at the time. It's going to be a firestorm when they find out – the police know, so they *will* find out. She says the insurance company probably won't pay out, so she'll be grounded forever. She's such an idiot! Anyway, tell me how you are! And have you read any more P and P?'

The very mention of Pride and Prejudice made Leo's hand clench. He made a huge effort to carry on the conversation normally, but his voice betrayed him, and Sophy interrupted. 'Leo, what's the matter? I can tell something's wrong! What is it?'

His attempts to brush it off as just being tired were ignored; she knows him far too well and he could hear her getting worried.

'Are you ill? Oh God, it's not something bad, is it? Please Leo, tell me! I know something's wrong.'

'I fell in love,' he said finally. She was nearly eighteen after all and they had probably covered every subject under the sun already, so why not tell her how miserable he was. He told her the whole story, ending with, 'And then she ran away.'

It took nearly three-quarters of an hour to cover the story itself and Sophy's comments and questions, but it comforted him slightly that she didn't try to minimize how he felt. He answered patiently, but it took an emotional toll to talk about it and once again he felt that he had failed, and it was not an emotion he was used to.

'And I know I shouldn't say this,' Sophy said just before they ended the call, 'but I'm glad you've told Sinda to bugger off! I've never told you about the way she talked to me that one time I met her, as if I was some kind of parasite, because *she* ran away from home at fourteen and has supported herself ever since. And she said I wasn't making the most of myself by hanging around at home letting you do everything for me and pay for every luxury I enjoy! I think she wants me out of the house because she hopes you'll marry her.'

'She isn't a nice person, poppet, and there's never been the slightest chance that I would marry her. We just go to events and openings together - she gets invited to everything and she often asks me to partner her. I've always known she could be a bitch, but to be fair she probably thought you were in your early twenties, as a lot of people do. You don't look anywhere near as young as you are when you're all dressed up with makeup on, you know that. But don't worry, I never was in love with Sinda and I'm not going to see her at all now, she's cooked her goose. And please do *not* mention to Mrs Campbell that

I'm not very happy or I'll have her fussing over me when I get home and it would drive me crazy.'

'Of course, I won't. I know she seems more like a mother or an aunt than a housekeeper sometimes, but we must have some privacy.'

He smiled. 'Quite right, poppet, sleep tight.'

He tidied up in the kitchen and loaded the dishwasher and thought he couldn't quite believe he told his baby sister the whole story. I really shouldn't have told her any of what Louisa said, he thinks guiltily, but it wasn't anything really personal, not like that stuff about Douglas, just that I know Jamie has got a nice job now in an eccentric bookshop and a safe place to stay. I'm glad Sophy didn't ask how I found that out, it would be a bit hard to explain, unless I lied and said Jamie told me herself.

Chapter 37

The reply from Jamie the next morning was brief and businesslike:

Thank you, I'll take up your offer of Derek's services, I'll contact him today. I trust him completely. Jamie

Leo sat in his office and stared at the phone for several minutes, read the brief message over and over and tried to pin-point the tone of it. Was there an unvoiced opinion at the end, something like 'as opposed to you'? Was she making it clear that she needed nothing more from him, that their shared concerns were now at an end? Or should he take it at face value, a simple statement of fact, nothing more and nothing less?

Derek's office was very tidy, there were no loose papers, everything was in folders, neatly stacked and perfectly lined up with the left-hand corner of his desk. Leo sat down in the chair opposite, still with the phone in his hand and stared out the window without focus. Derek glance up at him, read his thoughtful expression and left him to it while he finished the email he's writing.

'I just replied to the query from the Sullivan investment fund about the adjusted timeline to Stage One completion,' he said after a couple of minutes. 'I told them exactly what you told the board members the other day, which they knew already. I don't know why the Sullivan people don't read the board minutes - it was all very clearly laid out.'

'I know,' said Leo and smiled a tired smile. 'In every big project there seems to be one investor who feels they should be informed of everything on an individual basis, not in an update sent out to everyone involved. We've dealt with this kind of attitude before. I suppose they want to feel valued or important or something.' He held his phone out to Derek. 'Please read all the messages between Jamie and me.'

Derek didn't take the phone immediately, instead he looked closely at Leo as if he was making sure Leo really meant it.

'Take it!' said Leo roughly, and Derek took the phone and read the messages. Leo watched closely as he read, then scrolled back to start again from the beginning before he put the phone down without commenting.

'Do you mind? I promised you'd help her without asking you, but I thought you'd probably like to.'

'Of course, I'll do anything I can to help her, but I want to ask you something first – a couple of personal questions.'

Leo nodded and Derek thought for a moment and

when he spoke, he looked straight into Leo's eyes. 'What did you do? Or say? Why is she feeling that she's going to be seen as a gold digger or whatever you call that kind of opportunist? And what's all this stuff about Sinda? Suddenly you don't take her calls, I can't mention her name or pass messages on. How and why are these things related?'

Leo was silent for a long moment, his face unreadable, and then he sighed. 'Derek, I know I can trust you, but I have to say this first up. I'll tell you the story on the condition that you don't let Jamie know, or until she tells you herself. She's a very private person and she would hate to know I'm discussing this with anyone else, even with you. This is such a bloody mess!'

That's three people he had told now, he thought tiredly. But it couldn't be helped, this was too important to quibble over ethics. He told Derek a concise version of events. When he got to the bit about the phone conversation about Pride and Prejudice, Derek's eyebrows rose fractionally and there was a fleeting glint of amused surprise in his eyes. Leo continued with the call from Sinda that Jamie answered and the details of his own call to Sinda. He left out his conversations with Harriet and Louisa, and the fact that he had access to Jamie's laptop. Derek listened without a single interruption or question, and when Leo reached the end, he said. 'All right, I'll wait for her to call and then we'll sort it out. I'm sure there's a bolt cutter or a hacksaw somewhere on this site full of pickup trucks with big toolboxes on the back.'

He made no comment on the sad tale he had just

heard and didn't try to be comforting. He's a treasure, thought Leo, probably irreplaceable. God knows I might have cried if I'd been offered sympathy.

Sitting in front of Jamie's laptop that evening, Leo considered the potential consequences of his next actions. Soon he must turn the laptop off and put it back in the box in the guestroom wardrobe, but he was tempted to leave something of himself for her to find. He knew that most people would say that the logical and reasonable options open to him would be to either track her down, find her and hold onto her while he told her what that phone conversation was about, or email her, stating clearly that he knows what she must have overheard and explain it. But something inside him desperately wanted her to reconsider, to admit that she loved him, and even if she wouldn't spend any more time with him, to say 'I love you, but I don't trust you to be good for me.'

This strange feeling was more compelling than hunger or thirst; he needed her to be open with him, to ask for an explanation or to trust him to explain, without him having to force the explanation on her, even if it meant losing her before she had ever been his. He opened a blank Word document and wrote a poem, the first he had ever composed. When the file was saved as *Leo loves Jamie poem.docx* he took a deep breath and pressed the power button.

. . .

You've dismissed me out of hand, Jamie, he thought while he identified the box with 'laptop' among other things listed on the side. You didn't give me a chance, and though I understand your history now, I think you must make the first move, if we're going to have any chance at all. The thought, that if she didn't take that crucial first step, he might feel like he did now for the rest of his life, nearly choked him. He had never felt like this before.

———

Chapter 38

———

Early the following morning, Jamie called Derek to discuss what to do with the boxes.

'Of course, I can do that,' he said. 'There are plenty of tools around here, so getting that padlock off the storage unit is no problem, but why can't send me the key? Or is it maybe in one of the boxes?'

'Oh, God! I've done it again!' Jamie sounded as if she was on the verge of tears. 'Derek, my mind is still playing tricks on me, I just don't think straight sometimes.'

'Well, I would think it will do that for some time,' said Derek and made it sound quite reasonable. 'You've been badly concussed and under a lot of stress one way or another, so I'm not surprised. You've actually had two knocks to the head within a few weeks. You fell at that meeting in the school hall, remember? Mr Masters showed me the photo in the paper. You hear about people having trouble with memory and so on for a long time after a head injury and it's not really been very long at all, has it?'

There was a long silence at the other end and then she said slowly, 'Head injury? I never thought of it as a head injury, how odd – as if concussion wasn't a head injury. But of course, it is. You're probably right, Derek, you're so sensible, thank you! I've been getting better, but I still worry when things don't connect properly, or I forget something. One key to the padlock was in my car that got stolen and burnt, so that one's gone. But I do have a spare, it's in the box that says 'Miscellaneous' on the outside – in a little blue leather purse where I have all sorts of small things I don't want to misplace.'

'Consider it done, well, it will be in a few days. Don't forget to text the details of the storage place and the code, if I need one to get in. And how is life wherever you are? Mr Masters said you've found a place to live and a job.'

'Oh, Derek, it's the most wonderful place. A bookshop like something out of a story from the 1920's perhaps, or even Edwardian. Wood panelling, dark wood bookcases with finials on the corners and the most eccentric looking owner who dresses a bit like a country gent from the same era as the shop, but it is an act he puts on. He's famous and people come and take photos of him.'

'Are you happy?' asked Derek after a short pause, and Jamie was taken by surprise by the question which sounded as if he genuinely cared, he was not just asking out of routine, like when people asked, 'And are you happy in your new flat?'

'I'm OK, thanks.' And then, for some reason she couldn't quite understand, it burst out before she could stop herself, 'No, I'm not, Derek, I'm miserable!'

'So is Mr Masters – he's … I don't know what he is. I've never seen him like this in all the years I have worked for him. I hesitate to say it, Jamie, but I think his heart is broken.'

Tears welled over and ran down Jamie's cheeks, and she was silent for so long that Derek got worried. 'I apologise, I shouldn't have said that! It's not my business and I didn't mean to make you feel sad. Please forgive me!'

'Oh, Derek – it's so difficult. Do you mind if I tell you?' asked Jamie on a sob. 'You see, I heard Leo talking about me, I don't know who he was talking to, but it was about how I might be after – well, him or his wealth or something, conning him. And he sounded as if he didn't mind, as if it amused him. And then Sinda called and told me to get out of his flat and to crawl back into the gutter where I belong.'

She started to cry in earnest, speaking though sobs. 'Derek, I never cry – never! It's the concussion that's doing this to me, don't pay any attention. But you see, I was in a relationship for two years, when I was quite young, and it was so unbalanced, I loved him too much and he didn't love me enough.' She paused and blew her nose before she continued. 'And he was several years older than I was and very controlling. So, I was always on the back foot, always trying to be like he wanted me to be, but

I knew I never got it right, it was like I was constantly trying to justify my existence.'

'Oh, you poor thing! How did it end?'

'I had made a new friend, Louisa, she's years older than I am and my boyfriend didn't like her, and he kind of put obstacles in the way of my seeing her. Afterwards I realised that he knew she disapproved of him and how he treated me. And she's a strong woman, and that wasn't the sort of woman he liked me to have anything to do with. Well, he didn't really like me to have anything to do with anyone apart from him, now I think about it, I got very isolated. And then one day I had that kind of "on the road to Damascus" moment, just a blinding revelation and I saw the whole thing from the outside, if you know what I mean, like from an outsider's point of view. And I could see what he was doing, how he controlled me and disempowered me and isolated me. I was becoming like a slave, mentally. So, I called Louisa and then I packed my most important belongings in three bin liners and my sports bag, and she picked me up and I stayed at her flat until the end of my first year at university. I had just turned nineteen when I left him.'

She could hardly believe this outpouring to a man she had only met once, it was so unlike her, but for some reason she knew he would understand.

'And now you're worried that if you tell Mr Masters that you're fond of him, he'll think you are pretending, and you'll be back in that kind of relationship again?'

'Kind of, because he thinks I'm not being genuine, he

thinks I'm after something, so I would always be trying to prove that I'm not like that. But Leo isn't controlling like Douglas was. He's autocratic, but in a benevolent way.'

Derek chuckled. 'Perfect description! That's exactly how he is. He told me that he more or less abducted you for from the hospital and moved you to the private place and then from there to his apartment. Do you mind if I say something very personal?'

'God no! Derek, we're way past worrying about being personal, you know more about me now than nearly everyone in the whole world. I've just told you the most personal thing possible about myself, so don't worry.'

'When you left, you shut off communication, so instead of being in the same place and discussing these things, you're both locked into place way apart, waiting for something to unlock the situation, and neither of you is taking that first step - you're stuck. And it's hard taking the first step without being face-to-face or at least talking. Writing things isn't the same, it's too open to misinterpretation. You know, you can't hear the tone of voice or see the expression on someone's face. So, *you* are scared of being the underdog, if I can call it that. And Mr Masters feels he mustn't try to find you or tell you how it happened, if he doesn't understand you love him first, because he doesn't want to put pressure on you or make you feel you owe him anything. Maybe, if you could trust him enough to tell him you are miserable without him, or even that you love him, you can sort it out? Maybe something quite reasonable and innocent was behind that conversation you heard him have on the phone?'

'You might be right. Thank you, Derek – you're a darling, you really are. And I'm glad Leo has you to look after him. But I have to think about this before I do anything.'

'And by the way, just so you know. Sinda's been trying to patch it up with Mr Masters after he told her he'll never talk to her again. She's been calling me instead, because he's blocked her on his phone, and she told me she said nothing bad during that call with you – which I didn't believe. But he's forbidden me to mention her name, so I can't pass any messages on - not that I want to.'

After considering for half an hour Jamie picked up her phone and sent another long text message to Leo:

Leo, Derek told me that Sinda claims nothing bad was said during that call. I want you to know what she said, because I can't bear to think of you being with someone who lies to you. She told me to crawl back into the gutter where I came from, that she knew I had tricked you and I was after what I could get out of you, she called me a slut. It was vicious and aggressive, and it made me feel like a piece of rubbish. But I did manage to get a couple of hits in at the end. Jamie

Reply from Leo:

Dear Jamie, I have told Sinda that I never want to hear from her or see her again and if she spreads any rumours, I'll sue her. I am sorry she subjected you to such abuse. I wish you had stayed and told me that night, but as you chose to leave, I presume your feelings for me are not the same as mine for you. I do kind of understand. Leo. PS I think I have worked out what the hits were, but I might be wrong.

She read his message and sat for a few minutes with the phone in her hand, unable to get a grip on what she had just read and the implications. But slowly it meshed with what Derek said earlier, and something fell into place in her mind, she could picture it, the missing piece that had evaded her, the thing she must do to free him from this torment, which in a way was worse than her own. At least she had a choice, but he saw himself as without one. She wrote a message without re-reading it or even considering her choice of words as she usually did; she just wrote it and pressed Send.

Leo, being apart from you is like having a hole in my chest where my heart used to be. I don't know if we have any kind of future, but please know that I love you and there will never be anyone else for me. Jamie

She stared at message which now showed in blue, it had irretrievably gone, and Leo would have received it. She turned the phone off. Somehow sending that last message was the final straw, and now she felt as if she teetered on the brink of an emotional abyss. Whatever happened next would either be very good or very bad, and she didn't want to know right then when she was just about to go to work, or she might spend the whole day crying.

Chapter 39

The shop was surprisingly quiet, and Jamie was tidying old stock in the long, low-ceilinged storeroom upstairs.

'There's another thing that needs doing.' Bernard had come up to answer a couple of questions about where he wanted some old stationery stored, or if she should put it on the pile to go to the recycling depot. He pointed at a shelf low down. 'That white box is full of very old greeting cards and Christmas cards, just odds and ends. I've often wondered if they would be a nice thing to have on display somewhere, a curiosity, like an exhibition. I think the oldest must be from the 1920's but they could be even older. They were here when I bought the shop and I haven't looked at them for years, but perhaps you could go through them and pull out the interesting ones.'

Jamie carried the box, carefully balanced on her cast, down the narrow wooden steps from the loft and sat on the tall stool behind the counter to look through it, and before long she was immersed in musty-smelling treasures.

'There are lots of good ones,' she called out to Bernard who doing something at the far side of the shop. 'We could make a lovely display in the window and put them on Instagram and FaceBook - I bet people would like to buy them too, not just look at them. Some are probably collectors' items.'

'Let's have a look at them together later on and make some decisions,' said Bernard, and then the bell tinkled and a customer came in. Jamie was engrossed in the cards and didn't pay much attention to the conversation, until she heard Bernard say, 'I think you should go and talk to Jamie, she's at the counter over there. She'll be able to help you better than I can, I think.'

Jamie put a pile of cards back into the box and pushed it to one side as a tall girl in jeans and a red sweatshirt came towards her.

'Hi, I've got this project,' said the girl and pushed her long black braids back over her shoulders. She put her bag on the counter and fished around in it, lifted out a Kindle, a wallet and a phone, and finally a pad. 'I wonder if you have time to give me some ideas. Oh, sorry! I shouldn't show you this, not in a bookshop.' She pushed the Kindle quickly into the bag and Jamie laughed. 'I have one of those too, don't worry – it doesn't mean you don't like real books. And you're here, after all, it must mean something. Is it a school project?'

'No, it's my brother. I'm educating him.' She met Jamie's surprised look with a wry smile. 'I grew up in a strange household, well the first few years of my life anyway – very rough, I don't think I saw a book until I went to school. Our father was kind of anti-education and perhaps anti most things, I can't remember him at all, because he died when I was a baby. And our mother wasn't a reader, she drank a lot after my father died and then she died of pneumonia. Sorry, I shouldn't tell you all this personal stuff, but it's kind of the background to this project of mine. Now I love reading, and I'm having a fantastic education, and I want him to like books as much as I do!'

'What kind of books have you managed to get him to read so far?'

'Oh, masses of things. He's doing really well. I must say, I was disappointed when he refused to finish *Vanity Fair*, but he said he lost interest quite early on because Amelia Seddon is such a drip.'

Jamie laughed again and the girl grinned and continued, 'I know what he means and I get fed up with her too, but he *is* doing well. He loved *Life after Life*, you know that Kate Atkinson book, he said it wasn't just a great story, but it was clever as well. He likes clever books and books with lots of facts more than anything else. He likes Lee Child's books because of all the facts and information in them, and they're exciting. But I want him to read about people, too. People who are like real people, if you know what I mean? Not just hero type people, like Jack Reacher, so I thought I'd come in and ask for advice. I've brought the list of what I've given him to read so far.'

She held up the pad. 'On his next birthday I'm

planning to give him a card with a complete list of what he's read in a year and a row of gold stars.'

Jamie couldn't help smiling at her enthusiasm and energy. 'I know what you mean, that difference between books about what you call real people and hero type people. Probably boys relate more to heroes, but that kind of book might lead boys on to read other types of books too. How old is he?'

'Oh, he's a lot older than I am, it's just that he missed out on school, he left as soon as he legally could. But he's very interested in people. He often tells me funny details of what people say or do, he's very observant, more than most, I think.'

She frowned and looked down for a moment before she continued. 'Suggest something, please – about people, but clever too and a bit unusual. He's not happy right now, he's a bit down and I want to buy him a present and cheer him up, so nothing too tragic.'

Jamie came out from behind the counter and led the way to the modern fiction shelves, scanned them for inspiration and reached up for a copy of *The Time Traveller's Wife*.

'I don't know if this is likely to cheer him up, but it is very much about people and it's unusual in more ways than one, and a wonderful love story. Have you read it?'

'Oh, yes! I love it, and he's already got my copy of it. I bought it after my boyfriend's mother described it to me. And my brother said the sweetest thing when he'd finished reading it.' She got her phone out of her bag. 'You see my mother died when I was tiny, and he became my legal guardian even though he was only twenty-three at the time, and he's brought me up and looked after me ever since. And he sent me a text after he read it – hang on.' She unlocked her phone and scrolled through text messages while she talked. 'It's not very long ago, it will be easy to find. Oh, here it is. Read this.' And she handed the phone to Jamie.

"A bit like you and me, Poppet – only we're brother and sister, but the strange way it all happened, a bit like time travel? I had never lived in the same house with you and I hadn't seen you since you were a few months old and when I met you again, you were a little girl who came into my life like a surprise present. We're as good as any book, I think - and we always will be! Love you, Leo."

Jamie stood frozen with the girl's phone clutched in her hand, unable to think of anything to say, and after a moment she realised that she was crying.

'Oh, God! Please don't cry!' exclaimed the girl, dropped her bag with a thump and put both arms around Jamie and hugged her tight. 'Oh, *please* don't cry, I didn't mean to make you cry. I wanted to make it better, I know what happened and I found you. And Leo doesn't have a clue, he has no idea that I'm here. He thinks I'm at school in Bath - where we live.'

Jamie liberated herself and handed back the phone. Her tears had stopped as suddenly as they started, and she had no idea how she felt or what to say. They stood there behind the freestanding shelf with a card saying 'Politics' like two people immobilized by some cosmic force, the girl with her phone in her hand and Jamie with *The Time Traveller's Wife* still in hers. Then Bernard turned up beside them and said, as if this kind of drama was a common event in his shop, 'I think you two should go out and have a cup of coffee and talk it over, don't you? Take your time!'

Jamie stumbled off to pick up her bag. She still hadn't said a single word since she read Leo's text message and they said nothing as they walk side by side along the street, though Jamie could feel the girl glancing at her now and then. They went into the first café they saw and Jamie's only words were her coffee order. She headed for the nearest table, but the girl took her arm and steered her towards a corner. 'I think we need a bit of privacy, don't you?'

They waited in silence until their coffee arrived and then the girl reached out and put her hand on Jamie's. 'I'm so sorry, Jamie! I shouldn't have done it like that, I really didn't plan to spring it on you so suddenly. But when you picked out that particular book it felt as if it was meant, like fate was telling me to show you that message from Leo. I'm so worried about him, I've never seen him like this. He's on his knees, Jamie! Devastated that you left and he said he's failed you, he said he's never felt this way about anyone. Last night we talked on the phone for an hour, and he mentioned the quaint bookshop and I Googled it and found the one it must be.'

She stirred sugar into her coffee and pointed the

spoon at Jamie. 'And I bet you can't guess how many quaint, old-fashioned bookshops there are in England – dozens! But I reckoned it was probably this one because it isn't that far from Kingsbridge.'

While Jamie listened to this her brain seemed to have thawed. 'How did Leo know about the bookshop? Oh, never mind, maybe Derek told him.' In the back of her mind, she sensed that her reasoning was skewed, but she pushed the thought aside.

'Oh, probably, I didn't say how he knew. And by the way, my name is Sophy,' said the girl. 'Sorry, this is so back to front! I just came along to talk to you in case you … I don't know what I thought it might achieve. It was a mad thing to do, I know, but it couldn't get any worse, could it? And I love Leo more than anything in the world and I can't bear to see him so unhappy. He's always been there for me and he brought me up to be good and happy, and he's never let me down or put me second. He's the rock in my life and I know he will be forever. I had to try to help him!'

Jamie was silent for a moment and then she pulled her phone out, realised it was still turned off and turned it on. There was a new text message from Leo, she hesitated and put the phone down without reading it. 'This is a bit scary, Sophy. I sent a pretty revealing message to Leo this morning, laid it all out in the open. And then I couldn't bear to read what he might reply, because if it was really bad, I wouldn't have been able to cope at work, so I turned my phone off. And now he *has* replied.'

'And?' said Sophy and it was so like Leo that Jamie

had to smile. 'That's a familiar habit, that one-word question,' she said. 'Not that I really feel like laughing, I'm very nervous now. I was going to show you the message I sent him this morning, but now he's replied and I'm too scared to look.'

'Please read it, I promise I won't look while you read it.' Sophy pushed her chair back. 'I'll go and stand over by the counter.'

Jamie opened her text folder and her whole body was taut with stress; her hand shook. *That's exactly how I feel, can we talk? Leo*

Sophy was coming back with a plate of pastries in her hand and slowed before she reached their table, looked carefully at Jamie and broke into a smile. 'You look better!'

'I feel better, but not just because of his message. I've just understood something I heard him say, something that's been driving me crazy. My concussion is playing tricks on me and now and then I suddenly remember something or understand something. Did you tell him to read Pride and Prejudice?'

'Yes, but I don't own a copy, I read it from the school library, so he got a copy for his Kinde. And I know what you're thinking of. He told me how you must have heard us discuss Charlotte Lucas. He knows what you heard, he told me during that long phone call last night. He worked it out after a while, and he was shattered you thought he was mocking you or suspecting you of things. I'll tell you what he said: "I can't try to find her until I know what she feels, I could turn into a stalker". Do you understand it? I'm not sure I do, not really, but you look as if you do.'

She pushed the plate towards Jamie, who in turn pushed her phone across the table. 'You can read the last two – you might as well, you seem to know everything else already.'

Sophy read the messages and sighs. 'Oh! That's so lovely!' She picked up a pastry and bit into it and said with her mouth full, 'I hope someone sends me something so romantic one day! But what should I do now? I never thought this far – heavens! Should I tell him what I've done?'

Jamie felt as if she had not just suddenly gained a new friend, but been given responsibility for her, and she wanted to get it right.

'I need to think,' she said and smiled at Sophy's worried face. 'I'll eat my pastry while I think about it.'

After a pause she spoke again, and now she was decisive, certain that what she was saying was right. 'Sophy, I'll be forever in your debt for coming here and telling me what you did. It doesn't matter what Leo might think. You did something brave and beautiful and I love you for it. But you must tell him. If I tell him, it could be seen as me taking over, or you trying to avoid responsibility. You must tell him yourself, call him tonight, tell him what you did and text me when you've done it. I'll give you my phone my number. I'll call Leo straight after.'

Sophy nodded and keeps her eyes fixed on Jamie's

face, waiting for the next part which was clearly coming. 'And now,' said Jamie, 'I'm going back to work, and you're going to go back to Bath the way you came. Did you drive?'

'Oh no, I don't have a licence yet. I came by bus, well, two different buses, but it worked.'

'Have you got enough money? OK then.' They got up and Jamie reached out and pulls Sophy into a long, tight hug, then she stood back and smiled. 'I saw you with Leo in a restaurant in Kingsbridge, not so long ago. You look very different today!'

And Sophy laughed and made a funny face. 'I know, I recognised you straight away. It's such a joke when Leo takes me out for dinner sometimes with other people, businesspeople. I dress up in my very best gear and put on make-up and I do my hair all nice and wear perfume, and people think I'm his girlfriend! And then we laugh about it afterwards.'

'I did, I thought you were his girlfriend,' said Jamie, and Sophy reached out to take her hand. 'I hope this works out. You would be so great for Leo. And for me!'

'Only pay me for a half day,' said Jamie to Bernard, when she was back at the shop. 'I apologize for the drama and for leaving you in the lurch on a day when I'm your only helper! But I was taken totally by surprise, and it was something that had to be sorted out.'

'I think a bit of real-life drama is just what a bookshop needs every now and then,' says Bernard. 'But I would dearly like to know what caused this outpouring of emotion. Call me nosy, but I do love to hear about other people's lives.'

Jamie thought for a moment and said quite seriously, 'Charlotte Lucas from Pride and Prejudice got entangled in my life and very nearly wrecked it.'

She smiled at Bernard and went back to the old greetings cards and heard him say, as if to himself, 'Literature is such a dangerous commodity – it should come with a health and safety warning, it really should.'

It was late when Sophy called, and while Jamie waited, worried thoughts revolved in her brain like circling sharks. What if Leo was so angry with Sophy that it spilled over into her future relationship with him? Then she would have to help Sophy sort it out and it might not be a good start to the next stage of her relationship with Leo. When her phone buzzed, she reached for it so fast she dropped it on the bed and had to fumble for it.

'Hi, Jamie,' said Sophy, 'I've told him, but don't call him just now.'

And Jamie's heart did something very uncomfortable in her chest and she felt suddenly frightened. 'Why? Is he furious with you or with me?'

'Oh, no, no! He's not furious at all, he's *never* furious,' said Sophy with complete conviction. 'First, his phone was engaged and then when I finally got hold of him, he said he couldn't talk for long, he had to be available for a call about something important that he'd been waiting for

- a call from China, and he said it's *very* important, and it might go on for some time, because they're using interpreters, so it takes forever to get anything sorted out. So, he'll talk to me tomorrow. But I told him the gist of what I did, just briefly.'

Jamie put her phone on speaker and looked at the screen. 'It's nearly eleven now. Did you say I'd call him later, or do you think he'll call me?'

'He said for you to get some sleep and try not to have any nightmares, and he'll call you tomorrow, probably about lunchtime - and he said to tell you he loves you so much it hurts.'

Jamie was speechless at what seemed like an extraordinary thing for a man to say to his baby sister. 'He told you that?'

'He tells me everything,' said Sophy serenely. 'At least I think he does. I was four when Mum died, and he came and picked me up right away and took me home. He was living in a flat then, with only one bedroom, so we went straight out and bought one of those sofas that turn into a bed at night, so I had a bed. And we've talked about everything ever since.'

She giggled. 'I'm probably the only girl I know who tells her brother everything that goes on in her life. When I thought I'd probably have sex with my boyfriend, he just said, 'ok, but get on the contraceptive pill', so I did - but then I went off my boyfriend, so I stopped taking them.'

'You left them in the bedroom in Salcombe. They're still there.'

'Anyway,' said Sophy and picked up the thread again.

'When he came and took me away, he'd just started building up his business – he'd bought and sold things for a few years, since he was sixteen and then he bought a house. So, he rented it out and borrowed money from the bank and from some investor, who was impressed with him, and it just went on from there. I think he's really special, the way he makes people trust him.' She paused as if she was considering this statement for the first time. 'Anyway, that's what happens, everyone trusts him. And he changed my life, totally changed it like some kind of good fairy.' She started to laugh so hard she could hardly talk. 'I must remember to tell him that I think he's just like a good fairy. I'll say he's my hairy fairy - he'll be disgusted.' And she laughed again.

Jamie waited, smiling to herself and eventually Sophy controlled herself and continued. 'Do you want to know what it was like? Would you like me to tell you? Because it was so lovely and kind of like a story. I don't normally tell people, well, never actually, but I think maybe it would be good if you know.'

'If you don't mind talking about it, I'd like to know what it was like. I mean, he was only – what did you say this morning? Twenty-three?'

'Yes, he was twenty-three and he just turned up at my aunt's house and said, 'I've got legal custody and I'm taking her away'. And I put my red ball and my night dress and my toothbrush in a shopping bag, and we left. Just like that. He did ask me if I had favourite clothes or books or toys that I wanted to take, but of course I didn't. I didn't really have anything much. I'd never even held a book until I was in my aunt's house after mum died. And then we went and bought a whole heap of clothes and shoes and a teddy bear and some books, and later on he got me into a nice school and that was that.'

'It must have been so sudden – did it scare you to move away from everything you knew?'

There was a short pause, and Jamie hoped she hadn't triggered any traumatic memories for Sophy, but she could have saved herself the trouble.

'No, it was lovely,' said Sophy simply,' just lovely. You have no idea probably what it's like to live alone with a mother who's an alcoholic and spends all the welfare money on drink. And your home is filthy and you're too young to sort things out by yourself, like change sheets and wash clothes, and you often don't get a cooked dinner, well most of the time you don't. You eat crisps and bananas and maybe cold baked beans if you manage to open the tin. I think that that's why Leo learned to cook. He realised I'd never seen anyone cook a meal, you know, from scratch, so he started this habit of us shopping together and then cooking together. We still do, when he's home – well, Mrs Campbell cooks quite often too, of course. And Leo hadn't been in touch with the family for years, not since he was fifteen or sixteen when our dad beat him up so terribly that he ended up in ED, and he had to walk there. Just awful! But as soon as he heard my mother had died, he came straight away and got me. But of course, he didn't know me, and I didn't know him.'

'And you've lived with him ever since?'

'I have, and I've had the best upbringing ever. Leo is

like a brother and father rolled into one, but without the discipline bits, if you know what I mean. He just reasoned through things with me if I didn't behave, and he turned up at school concerts and school sports and I had a normal childhood – well, minus the first four years of course.'

When they ended the call, Jamie got into the striped PJ's and lay awake for a long time considering the call from Sophy and what she had leant about Leo. A lot of what she had found unusual about him had been explained by Sophy's story, things like how decisive he was and how caring and kind. She couldn't wait to talk to him.

Chapter 41

The shop phone rang just before lunch, and Jamie looked over to see if Bernard or Robbie was closer to the counter than she was. Bernard got there first and stood looking down at the counter while he listened and after a couple of minutes, he said, 'Yes, of course – have you got a pen?' He read out a cell phone number and said goodbye.

Jamie was waiting to ask if he would have time to look at the old cards this morning, but he interrupted her halfway through her question. 'Sorry, but I've got to go out for a few moments, back soon!' He picked up his cell phone from under the counter, walked through the back room and disappeared out into the yard.

Robbie looked after him with a grin. 'That was pretty secretive. Do you think he's hooking up with someone?'

Jamie smiled, made no comment and walked away to start unpacking a box of new books in the back room. She was thinking about what kind of car she might get now that the insurance money had finally come through, and who might give her good advice.

Leo, she thinks, of course he'll know, he seems like a car man. Or Derek, no point asking Louisa, she wouldn't have a clue and Gemma would just say 'get a big one in case you're in an accident', which is what she said when I bought the Polo.

Bernard came back inside a few minutes later, and they looked at the new books together and decided how many of each to put on the shelves in the shop. 'And the cards – we could look at them now, or I could put the ones I think are particularly interesting in a separate box. I think it will take a bit of time to go through them.'

'Put them in a box for now,' said Bernard and started picking up books to take out to the shop. 'And then, if you wouldn't mind, could you go down to the café on the corner to the right - the one with the old-fashioned sign with gold script - and buy some nice cakes for afternoon tea? Perhaps custard squares? It's a special day today and a little celebration would be nice, I think. Take some money out of the till.'

Jamie took a five-pound note from the till and said, 'I'll be back soon,' to Robbie, who was up on a stepladder dusting the top of the shelves.

The sun had come out after a grey morning, and she turned right with the sunshine warm on her back and headed down towards the corner. Halfway there her phone buzzed with a call and she stopped to check it, a call from Leo. Her heart speeded up and she felt breathless, her fingers were clumsy when she swiped up.

'Jamie,' said the voice that she had only heard in a voice message since she left Salcombe. 'Turn around, darling.'

Confused, she turned, and there he was, right behind her, and she stared at him as if he were a ghost. He took the phone out of her limp hand and put his arms around her, and she leaned against his chest and closed her eyes.

'Jamie, please tell me we're going to be OK,' he said.

'Oh, we *are*,' said Jamie with great certainty and tilted her head back to look up at him. 'We're going to be *way* more than OK.'

'I feel like never letting you out of my sight again.' He took her hand and slid it in under his jacket. 'Can you feel my heart? It's back in my chest again.'

She stood on tiptoes to kiss him. 'Thanks to Sophy.'

He shook his head, as in disbelief, but there was a smile lurking at the corners of his mouth. 'When she rang last night and told me what she had done, I couldn't believe it. But I'm so proud of her − the initiative! But I think we would have made it anyway. Once I got that text message about the hole in your chest, I knew I'd be able to explain to you. And there's no way that damn Charlotte Lucas is getting an invitation to our wedding.'

Jamie stared at him as if she didn't understand the words, and then she started to laugh. 'Wedding − really?'

'Why are you laughing? It's no laughing matter, getting married is a serious thing. I don't know how soon it can happen, but let's find out.'

He meant it and she couldn't think of a single reason not to agree. 'You're right, I was just surprised. I'm sorry I laughed! Of course, we'll get married, any time you like.'

And then she remembered the phone. 'Oh no! Where's my phone? I had it in my hand and then …'

'In my pocket, with mine,' said Leo. 'You looked as if you were about to drop yours and I needed both hands free. Let's go and have lunch!'

'But I must do my errand first.' Jamie had just remembered where she was going. 'I'm buying cakes for afternoon tea. Bernard said he's got something to celebrate, it's probably his birthday.'

'We'll bring some cakes back after lunch. That errand was just a way to get you out of the shop and heading in the right direction so I could come up behind you. Bernard and I worked it out on the phone just now, and he doesn't expect you back until later this afternoon, it's all arranged. He thinks the whole thing is wonderful, he said the things that have happened in the shop since he hired you are better than any novel.'

It was Jamie's turn to shake her head. 'I can't believe you planned all that instead of just walking into the shop – you're so lovely!'

'I wanted to set the scene for proposing, not that I did it very well,' said Leo and took her hand. 'But you've accepted now, and if you try to get out of it, I'll sue you for breach of promise. And now, let's go and have lunch at my hotel where we can look at the view and be out of this wind.'

Chapter 42

Twenty minutes later Jamie looked out over the sand dunes and the sea. "This is a gorgeous place for a hotel. I haven't had time to look around the town properly yet. I started working for Bernard practically the moment I got here and it's only a couple of days ago. Incredible! Are you staying here for the night?'

'*We* are staying here tonight, in a room upstairs with a splendid view, and tomorrow ...' He stopped talking and looked suspiciously at her. 'Yes?'

'Yes, what?'

'You got that look on your face just then – I have a feeling you're going to tell me off.'

'I was wondering if you had already organized my exit from Torquay in your usual autocratic fashion. Have you resigned me from the bookshop, cancelled my room and packed my clothes again?'

He studied her face for a moment to make sure that

she wasn't serious and then he smiled. 'No, I haven't done any of those things. But I was going to say that tomorrow I have to go back to work, and I thought you might come back with me.'

She rose and walked around to his side of the table, and bent down to kiss him. 'Of course, I'll come with you, you couldn't leave me behind if you tried! And you can be as autocratic as you like, I'll just have to learn how to hold my own when I need to.'

'Will there be anything else?' asked the waiter when they had finished lunch. 'Coffee perhaps?'

'No thanks,' said Leo without consulting Jamie. 'We haven't got much time.'

She walked ahead of him out of the dining room and headed for the lift, which she spotted on the way in, and Leo put his arm around her shoulders. 'You read my mind.'

'I've been reading your face right through lunch, Leo! I was worried you'd focus too long on something and start a fire.'

'I wrote you a poem,' said Leo, sounding as if were making a confession, as they walked along the corridor to his room. 'I wrote it when I was really sad and worried, and it's not very good, but I'll give it to you because I wrote it on your laptop and it's saved there, so you'll find it one day anyway.' He pulled a folded paper out of his pocket, a piece of hotel stationery. 'Here it is.'

Jamie unfolded it as soon as they are inside the room, read it and her eyes filled with tears. 'You are such a wonderful man, and I'm so sorry I left like that, but I just had to.'

'I know, I understand it now.'

She leaned against him and read the poem again and thought there couldn't possibly by another man like him in the whole world.

My world is empty, the sky is grey.
I need you here to love each day.
My heart feels hollow, I'm on my knees.
Darling Jamie, come back please!

An hour later, Jamie looked at Leo, who was lying on his back with his eyes closed. 'What are you doing? Are you falling asleep?'

'No, I'm just enjoying being happy and thinking, and planning the future. I can't do it with my eyes open, not when you're right next to me with no clothes on, I'll get distracted.'

'But before you decide on the future of the universe, please tell me that Sophy's truly forgiven. She was worried you'd be annoyed that she had interfered, but personally I think she should be given an award.'

'I always forgive Sophy. She's been living with me since she was four, and I'm so proud of her, Jamie. She had a terrible start in life, neglect and deprivation – and I didn't even know! I hadn't been near my mother for years, not since I was sixteen, apart from a very brief visit when my dad died and Sophy was about three months old. My home life was bad enough, but the way it hit rock bottom after my father died, and the poor little thing had to cope as best as she could. As soon as I heard my mother had died, I went straight back and picked Sophy up. I told my aunt I was her legal guardian, but I didn't actually get that sorted until a couple of months later. It was more complicated than I'd thought it would be. When I realised what her life had been like, I felt so guilty – if I'd gone back earlier, I would have discovered. So, I wanted to give her a decent home, a proper home, and bring her up to be good and have solid values.'

'All the things you missed out on,' said Jamie. 'The things you had to teach yourself as you grew up. You've done a great job with Sophy, she's lovely – and you've done a fantastic job on yourself, too.'

Leo turned his head to look directly at her. 'I thought I was going crazy when you left. I worried about you not being safe and about you having nightmares without me there to comfort you and if you had enough money – everything!'

'It was awful for me too, but at least I wasn't worried about your safety, like you were about me. And how *did* you work it all out?'

He rolled onto his side and his face was right next to hers, their noses were nearly touching. 'This is the truth,

Jamie. Too late now for you to pull back, so I'll tell you how I worked it all out. I stopped at *nothing*. I discarded my principles, told lies, invaded your privacy and used everyone I could lay my hands on without the slightest hesitation. And I'm looking forward to meeting my chief co-conspirator very soon. In fact, the sooner the better. I think we're going to get along extremely well.'

Jamie studied his face and waited, certain that he wouldn't be able to resist surprising her without her having to ask, but he looked back, deadpan and silent, and after a moment she gave in. 'Meeting? So, it's someone you've never met?'

'I've only talked to her on the phone a couple of times – oh, and one email. But those conversations were very long and *very* personal, so I feel I know her really well already. Louisa, your friend Louisa.'

'What?! How did you know about her, how did you find her?'

'As I said, I invaded your privacy. Your laptop was on, in sleep mode and plugged in, that's how you left it. I read a couple of emails and decided Louisa was a key person in your life and sent her a message from my own email account.'

There was a long moment of silence and then Jamie started to laugh. 'I have sometimes wondered how you got to where you are – and never more so than now that I know your background, but ...'

'But?'

'Oh, nothing. I just understand it now, all the pieces just have fallen into place in my mind.'

'And are you going to tell me what that means? Is it good or bad?'

'It's totally fabulous and amazing,' said Jamie seriously. 'I'm the luckiest woman in the world.'

Many Thanks

We hope you've enjoyed reading this story and would consider leaving a review on your favourite review site, or with the retailer you purchased from.

These are not only much appreciated, they also help other readers discover new authors.

For more about other titles in this series, please read on.

Letters from the Past

Letters from the Past is a series of stand-alone novels where a letter from or about the past reveals something that changes a woman's perceptions of herself or of her family, and that affects her outlook on life.

These books are such fun to write, and I am always working on the next title in this series. I hope you will enjoy reading them as much as I enjoy writing them!

Tina

Having had nobody in her life since her husband died, Lara unexpectedly finds herself involved with three men. One is planning to use her, one she plans to use for her own ends, and one becomes a "friend-with-benefits" with surprising results. Sometimes a quiet schoolteacher is not all she seems at first glance.

Callista experiences an event of apparent ESP at the Okehampton Castle ruins and becomes a media sensation, but the effect it has on her life is dramatic. How do two people, one calm. one seriously claustrophobic, who feel they are poles apart, cope for an hour and a half in total darkness in a stalled lift? And can they handle the consequences?

Sofia's life is in turmoil: a difficult diva mother, a letter with a confession about a family killing and having to accept help from a man she loathes when she is injured. Can reluctant attraction turn into love?

Who is the stranger living in the empty house Miranda inherited from her grandmother? Why is he living like a secretive recluse in someone else's house? Reckless Miranda decides to confront him, and what she discovers prompts her to set out on a fearless quest to bring justice to a man who has given up hope. But is the gamble too great or a risk worth taking?

When Emma finds an old letter in a library book she is instantly intrigued, but by researching the origin of the letter she unwittingly opens the door to danger and becomes the target for threats and harassment. Nearly desperate, she takes a leap of blind faith into the unknown and accepts an offer of help from a stranger - but can she trust him?

Jamie, an ardent protester against the gigantic Vista Resort development and Leo Masters, the high-powered developer, seem unlikely to ever agree on anything. But unexpected coincidences and chance brings them together in a fragile state of mutual respect. Will courage and kindness resolve the situation, or do they need help?

After a bizarre accident with ESP overtones, the media haunt Arapera. But can she trust an offer of help from a man she has only met once? Or will she regret it for the rest of her life if she doesn't take the chance? Sometimes life is a knife-edge balance between staying safe and taking risks, and there is no way of predicting if the gamble is worth it.

When crime-writer Saskia finds an unconscious stranger, she has a strange and strong emotional connection. Pretending to be his cousin and with no thought for the consequences, she spends weeks at his hospital bedside. But what will happen when he wakes and discovers she has invaded his life, breached his privacy and made crucial decisions on his behalf?

Also by Tina Clough

THE GIRL WHO LIVED TWICE

What would you do if you woke up one morning and found that time had rewound exactly a year? Would you revisit your past mistakes and try to do better? Would you try to get revenge on those who had wronged you? Or would you use what you knew to get rich? When Mia finds herself in her own past, she must decide how best to use her pre-knowledge of one year's worth of events and personal issues.

RUNNING TOWARDS DANGER

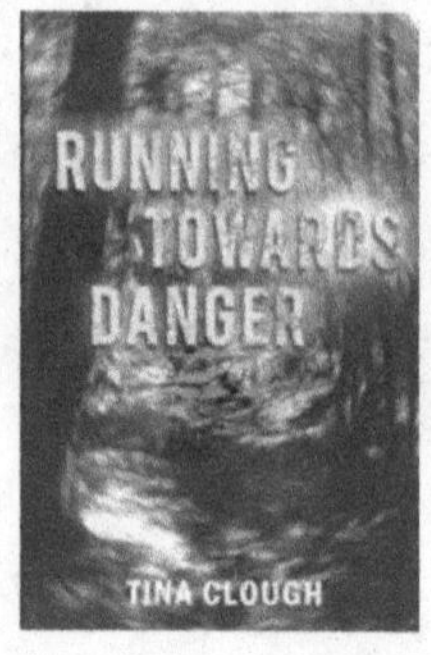

When Karen's flat-mate Nick is gunned down in front of her in the street her life is turned upside-down. Everything she thought she knew about him turns out to be a lie. She becomes a suspect in the police investigation and drug bosses think she knows where Nick has hidden a large sum of money. When her life is threatened, she decides to leave town and disappear.

Karen becomes Cara and creates an anonymous existence, severs all links to her past and adopts a cash-based way of life that leaves no electronic traces. But despite her careful planning danger still stalks her and she is forced to make dramatic choices in the face of threats and brutal violence.

Can she trust the man she is attracted to, or has he been sent by the killers to gain her confidence and find the money they believe she has?

THE CHINESE PROVERB

Book 1 - Hunter Grant Series

Army veteran Hunter Grant thought he had left war behind in Afghanistan – a conflict that left him with physical and psychological scars.

But finding an unconscious girl in the Northland bush and gradually untangling her story involves him in warfare of a different kind in his own country.

Hunter sets out to find and punish the man Dao calls Master, but he soon finds there is more to this story than enslavement. Before long he himself is being hunted by the overlord of a drug empire whose sole objective is to kill Dao because she knows too much.

Protecting her and waging war while trying to keep the police from stifling his enterprise takes all Hunter's ingenuity and determination and puts him in deadly jeopardy.

ONE SINGLE THING

Book 2 - Hunter Grant Series

Journalist Hope Barber disappears two weeks after returning to New Zealand from an assignment in Pakistan, leaving her front door open and her bag and phone inside. The police are tight-lipped about their reluctance to act, and Hunter Grant and Dao agree to help Hope's brother Noah find her. Details about Hope's time in Pakistan gradually emerge but only raise more questions.

Was Hope under surveillance?

Was she linked to terrorists?

And who is the man Hope called 'my stalker'?

THE SHADOW BROKER

It is 2026 and individual freedoms are severely curtailed, with state surveillance everywhere. State Security has a Watch List, and being on it means that nothing you do or say escapes the authorities, but does the Kill List really exist? And if it does, how would you know if you were on it?

Coded messages on a found burner phone, top-level government corruption and a shadowy mastermind who calls himself The Broker. In this climate of state control, three unlikely friends start quietly looking for connections and set in motion a deadly game of hide and seek that will change their lives forever.

Trying to uncover the truth means risking your life, and nothing is more dangerous than searching for evidence of government corruption.

About the Author

Tina Clough grew up in Sweden and now lives in New Zealand; dividing her time between writing fiction and translating and editing medical research papers.

Between working and writing she looks after an acre of fruit trees, vegetable gardens and roaming hens.

Apart from reading her interests include photography, wine, growing organic vegetables, making jam and kayaking.

https://lightpoolpublishing.com